The Warrior

by
Ty Patterson

The Warrior

by
Ty Patterson

Books by Ty Patterson

Warriors Series

The Warrior, Warriors series, Book 1
The Reluctant Warrior, Warriors series, Book 2
The Warrior Code, Warriors series, Book 3
The Warrior's Debt, Warriors series, Book 4
Flay, Warriors series, Book 5

Sign up to Ty Patterson's mailing list,
http://eepurl.com/09nyf, and get The Warrior, free. If you
tick the Launch Team check box, you will receive beta-read
copies of all my new releases in advance, free.

Praise for The Warrior

What a ride — Christine Terrell, Goodreads

What a great book! It has been a long time since I have had a book keep me on the edge!

I believe Ty Patterson is the next up and coming thriller writer

The Warrior Rocks

Ty Patterson is now added to my favorites list

A must read!

Intense – No Better Way of Saying It

Zeb Is My Hero! If Only He Were Real

What an awesome book!

A real page turner!

Gripping Read

A must read for anyone who enjoys a well told story

Acknowledgements

Donna Rich for her proofreading, Pauline Nolet for her proofreading and editing, (www.paulinenolet.com),Jason & Marina Anderson of Polgarus Studio (www.polgarusstudio. com), for formatting.

Dedications

To my wife who challenged me, and my son
who inspired me.

Chapter 1

He lies in the moonless night, waiting.

He came to the village just as dusk settled in, and has become one with the rainforest. The mud huts with thatched roofs are just about a hundred yards away, so close that he can hear conversations in the huts, families eating, children crying, and women cooking. The village is split by a road going through it, with huts almost evenly scattered on either side of it, about two hundred of them in all. He knows from his reconnaissance file that there is a concrete structure in the middle of the village that serves as a communal school and youth center.

He observes the arrival of the soldiers close to midnight, about forty of them in two trucks and an open-topped Jeep, a few white-skinned among them. He hears them banging through huts, the screams of women and children, sounds of violence, and the occasional shots.

He calls Andrews on his satellite phone.

'Shit has happened. Forty-odd soldiers drove in half an hour back. I can't see what's happening, but I can hear women and children screaming, and shooting. I'm going in.'

'No!' Andrews shouts across continents. He pauses for a moment, gathering his thoughts. 'Don't engage. Observe, record, and report was your remit, and still is. Are those FDLR soldiers?'

'Wearing those uniforms. A few white-skinned in them as well. Haven't a clue if they're the real deal or not,' he replies. 'I can get up close and personal and find out if I go in.'

Andrews laughs harshly. 'I know what that means. You are not going in whatever happens. I'll call their embassy in Washington as well as our embassy over there and alert them. BUT YOU ARE STAYING PUT.' His voice rises with each word.

He lets Andrews stew in the ensuing silence for a long while till Andrews breaks.

'I know what you want to do, but trust me on this. You are a more valuable asset outside than inside despite whatever shit is raining down there.'

He hangs up on Andrews and continues observing, blackness coiling deep inside him.

He starts the tabla in his head to drown out the anguish of

the women and children, and forces his mind to play various *taals*. He is on the *teentaal* when the trucks finally roar off filled with the soldiers; the voices of the women and children mute a little, but not by much.

The Jeep is still there, its front just peeping out from the shadow of a hut. He silences his mental tabla and listens. Ghostly shadows move between the huts occasionally. If sound could be blotted, it would be a lazy evening in the Congo.

* * *

Zeb is a specialist, a troubleshooter – a private military contractor if you want to be nit-picky.

In an earlier life, he was with the US Special Forces. Some would say he is a mercenary. He is hired around the world for his skills in finding things. Things such as stolen nuclear warheads or terrorists. He is also hired for finding people: hostages kidnapped for ransom, soldiers held prisoner in enemy territory, civilians held hostage by wackos – finding anyone, really.

He has often acted as a bodyguard, security consultant, or protector. Sometimes he is hired to make people disappear. Bad people, roaches. Some call him an assassin. He knows he isn't one, but can do that job better than the best assassins in the world. Labels don't bother him. His job is a violent, high-risk one. He wouldn't do it if it wasn't.

Armed forces across the world hire him, as do police forces, national governments, Hollywood stars, and billionaires.

* * *

His last assignment had been to retrieve a stolen Russian nuclear warhead.

He had to work with the agency as well as various covert government organizations in Europe, the USA, and Russia, infiltrate a few terrorist cells, and negotiate with the world's most wanted arms dealers before locating the warhead in a mosque in Detroit. He had then called in the agency, who in turn had called a few WDE (We Don't Exist) organizations to conduct a dawn raid on the mosque. He was part of the team that went in; it was his finger that pulled the trigger splattering the brains of two members of the cell.

He had flown to New York for his debrief at one of the several anonymous offices maintained or temporarily occupied by various federal agencies.

Andrews was waiting for him in the colorless office. 'We have something else for you, if you're interested.'

That was Andrews. Good at small talk.

'But first things first,' continued Andrews. 'Report?'

He wordlessly handed it across. He had worked with Andrews for a long time, could easily read him, and he knew Andrews wasn't really interested in his report. He would have been thoroughly debriefed by the WDE agents. Andrews was here to stoke his interest in the next assignment, whatever it was. Andrews was a first-rate handler who gave him interesting assignments, and for that he could tolerate his boring games. For a short while.

Andrews finally put the report down, drummed his fingers on the desk, looked at him, then away and then back at him. 'We might have a problem.' He paused. 'In the Congo.'

Andrews waited for his response. Realizing it could be a long wait, he continued. 'As you know, the Democratic Republic of the Congo (DRC) has a UN Peace Keeping Force (UNPKF), which has not been particularly effective in keeping the peace. In fact, the UNPKF has been accused of not doing enough to keep out rebel troops and of being involved themselves in drug and gold smuggling.'

Andrews waited for a response, got none, and forged ahead. 'But the UN Force is not what's troubling us. There are a bunch of military contractors out there, gone to train the DRC's army. Six of them. The agency has used them in the past but stopped dealing with them. Too brutal. Don't play by the unwritten rules in our game. They deal with multiple paymasters at the same time, and some of those paymasters are the bad guys. That's bad with a B. Folks we would terminate. Hence the agency blacklisted them. Now over the past few months there have been whispers of military contractors actively working with the other side, the Democratic Forces for the Liberation of Rwanda.'

Andrews snorted. 'Democratic Forces for the Liberation of Rwanda, aka FDLR. That's the French name for them. And don't even ask me why a force for the liberation of Rwanda is active in the DRC, but they are, and are fighting the DRC government troops, who we are backing.'

'So?' Zeb prompted.

'The chatter is that these contractors are not just working with the FDLR, but have gone rogue. Now the fucking thing is we haven't a clue if these rogue contractors are the ones who went to train the DRC troops. The intel is not the most reliable out there. The agency blacklisted those six, but it would be a political minefield if the rogue contractors turned out to be the six the agency used in the past. China is expanding its presence in Africa, and we want to be seen as the good guys. We want you to go to the DRC, find out who those guys are and what the fuck they're up to. No action. Just investigate and report.'

'Nope.'

Andrews waited for an explanation, got none, and did his routine of looking away and back, and drumming his fingers. 'Yes, I thought you'd say that. Not challenging enough for you, I expect. Hang on a second – I want you to meet someone,' he said and slipped out of the room. He came back with the Director.

And then it became personal; Andrews knew Zeb couldn't refuse the Director. The Director and Zeb's sister went back a long way, and the Director never hesitated to draw on Zeb's goodwill bank if she had to.

* * *

Zeb has been in the Democratic Republic of the Congo for a couple of months now under the guise of a charity worker. He has worked in remote villages and steadily moved his way from Kinshasa in the west, to North and South Kivu in the east.

He has travelled by train, boat, and ridden carts and donkeys. He has gone drinking with the Congolese, helped thatch huts and build schools, all the while keeping his ears open for gossip on foreign contractors. Information has been surprisingly easy to come by. The aid workers and the Congolese are all too happy to have a sympathetic ear after all the years of inhuman brutality.

The history of the Democratic Republic of the Congo has been one of civil war and corruption right from its independence in 1960. It has witnessed army mutiny, armed rebels backed by Rwanda and other neighboring countries, turning the country into a vast battleground, all fuelled by a thirst for the country's rich natural resources.

There are numerous mercenaries in the Congo. Some of them South African, some Belgian, a few British and American, and many other nationalities. He has met a few of them. Most of them have been hired for the protection of villages, as bodyguards of businessmen or politicians, or for protection of business assets. Some offer security consultancy to various government bodies and businesses.

It's in Kindu – almost in the center of the DRC – that he first hears of a group of contractors who have gone to the other side. The Congolese who mention them are fearful and whisper about mass rape and these contractors in the same breath.

'La mal personnes' and *'atrocities'* are the words they use to describe the contractors. After many Ngok and Primus beers over several days, he hears that the contractors and the FDLR soldiers they are associated with, are now based near Lake Kivu, near the border with Rwanda.

He isn't surprised at the ease of gathering this intel – it's not easy for six white men to blend in with black soldiers. They would be easily noticed.

The Congolese say these men capture and loot mines, often killing mine workers in the process. Small-scale mining is widespread in the DRC, and because of their size, it's very easy for armed bands of men to hijack the mines.

The FDLR soldiers and the white-skinned contractors take the mines over and trade in gold, minerals, diamonds, and ivory – anything that has value. They prey on the local villages for food and women. The DRC's army and police are either incapable or unwilling to deal with the problem or, more likely, are in collusion with the criminals. The UN Peace Keeping Force is usually too late to the scene and stretched too thin.

On a few occasions, he meets victims who have suffered at the hands of this renegade band of thugs. They all speak of the ruthlessness of the soldiers, both black and white. He records his conversations with the Congolese victims and pretty soon has a dossier of atrocity. A few victims have even identified the mercenaries from their agency photographs he carries. He has decided to visit a few villages in North and South Kivu before making his way back to Kinshasa and then back to the US.

* * *

And this was how he came to be lying in wait on the outskirts of Luvungi, one of the villages in the vicinity of Lake Kivu. This is the third village near Lake Kivu that he has surveilled.

It's been a couple of hours since the trucks left, the jeep is still there, and nothing has changed. He doesn't know how many soldiers have gone in the trucks or how many have been left behind.

He's going in.

It isn't in him to be a passive spectator. Andrews can go fuck himself.

The rainforest comes almost to the edges of the village, with plenty of foliage to give him cover. He decides to start with the hut on the extreme right and make his way to those on his left where the Jeep is parked.

He centers himself and drifts from shadow to shadow towards the perimeter of the village. Some of the huts are dark; some are lit from within by lamps, candles, or burning ovens, throwing a mosaic of light and shadows on the ground outside the huts. No movement that he can see. He sidles around the side of the first hut and peers through the door, his body masked by the wall.

Nothing.

Something cooking in the oven, but the hut is empty. The next hut is empty too, and so are the next ten. He goes to the next row of huts closer to the road. He can hear a woman wailing inside, another voice murmuring something. He peers inside. A woman, barely clothed, is lying on the mud floor, her mouth and forehead bleeding, a wash of blood down her thighs. Another woman is pressing a wet cloth to her head.

He stills even more, his pulse slowing, his mind going into the familiar grey fog, preparing the body for wreaking violence. Extreme violence. The next hut is empty, and after a quick glance, he moves on. Something tugs at the edge of his vision, making him return to the hut and look again, more carefully this time.

There, just near the oven, something familiar and yet not. He steps inside and sees a baby, maybe six months old, lying close to the fire, her hand outstretched towards the coals. He hunches down and puts his ear to her chest. Her heart is beating. He moves her farther from the fire, puts it out, and ghosts out.

The next hut, a young girl raped, alone and unconscious; another hut, an old woman beaten and bleeding, lying on the ground, her clothes barely covering her body, moaning softly. She sees him with blank eyes, but does not register his presence.

He crosses the road to the huts on the other side, figuring to search the huts on both sides of the road, behind the Jeep. The first hut he looks into shelters a young girl, maybe seven years old, lying on her side facing the door. The stench of blood and burning hair fills the hut. Her long hair trails behind her and ends in the oven. He scoops the remaining hair out of harm's way, kills the fire, and kneels beside her. Her dark, empty eyes regard him with weariness as she rolls on her back, thighs spread.

Looking down at her, Zeb allows the rage to blossom, unfurling from its controlled core within, reaching out across his body to his extremities, making him the most efficient killing machine on earth. The little girl's vacant eyes follow him as he leaves the hut.

Next hut, scuffling and grunting from within. White male, nearly six feet tall, pinning a young girl to the floor, simultaneously raping and strangling her.

The blackness in him is lightning fast as he grabs the man by his collar, flings him back against the wall, and holds him there.

Jason Boulder, ex-Delta, ex-Iraq, Somalia, and now here. Zeb recognizes him from Andrews' dossier. Boulder looks at him in disbelief and is about to yell out when Zeb's blade severs his carotid. Zeb rolls the body on its belly to lie on its spurting blood and spreads a tattered blanket over it. All this in just a few seconds, with the girl not fully comprehending what has happened.

He slips out of the hut and pauses in the shadows to take stock. Still the same: women wailing, others consoling them, no one running in his direction, and no bullets fired at him. No male villagers visible.

He quickly checks all the other huts in that row and discovers more carnage, more blank eyes, but no other soldiers or mercenaries. It takes him another hour to go through all the huts on that side of the road before he heads toward the huts where the Jeep is parked. He figures there must be about two hundred women beaten and raped – many of those young girls. His iPhone memory is nearly full from the pictures he has taken, and he makes a mental note to transfer those to Andrews when he has a good connection.

He doesn't know how many soldiers have stayed behind or

whether the mercenaries he is seeking are here. The only clue he has is Boulder's presence.

The Jeep might have some answers.

The Jeep is parked on the central road in the village, with four huts on either side of the road in front of it. All those huts are lit from within, throwing the vehicle into sharp focus. He moves along the far row of huts, towards the driver's side, keeping an eye on the Jeep and at the same time checking out the huts. In some of these huts he sees some men shot and dead. They account for the shots he has heard. Still, for a village of this size there should be more men about, and their absence bothers him. Maybe they weren't in the village when the trucks arrived, or they were carted off in the trucks by the soldiers.

He tucks this mystery at the back of his mind and concentrates on the Jeep and the huts in its immediate vicinity. After clearing the huts in his row, he lies prone in the deepest shadow and looks at the Jeep from the corners of his eyes to see if he can detect any movement. He takes a risk and runs at a half crouch toward the Jeep, keeping out of its windshield's sight line. The Jeep is a standard FDLR vehicle, battered but serviceable, with its keys still in it. He is tempted to pocket the keys but squelches the thought. Not knowing the strength of the soldiers left in the village, he doesn't want to give his presence away.

He looks across the driver's seat towards the other row. He thinks he hears some murmuring above the women's anguish, but he isn't sure.

He crouches and runs towards the row of huts. The first of the four is empty. The next one has a woman facing the door, and when he peeks around the opening, her eyes widen and her mouth opens. All she can feel is a rush of air as he flows across the hut, clamps his hand over her mouth, squeezes a pressure point on her carotid, and renders her unconscious. He gently lowers her into a shadowed corner and moves on to the next hut.

This is where he can hear the murmuring louder. He goes around the rectangular hut to see if he can peer through a crack in the wall, but there is none. The hut has two windows on the two opposite walls, and peering through them would illuminate his face.

Over the years of working as a PMC with the agency, he

has amassed exotic gadgets, from shoe-heel cameras to bug-sized remote-controlled robots. He unsheathes a meter-long slender cable from the leg of his fatigues. One end of the cable has a USB plug and the other end a self-focusing twenty-megapixel camera. The iPhone is its power source. He plugs the cable into his iPhone, loops the camera through a corner of the window, and watches its feed on his phone.

Two white males, one with his back to the door, the other sideways, are squatting beside an almost naked woman. She is still, and he can't tell if she is unconscious, dead, or too frightened to move. The men are counting something. One of them is stuffing what looks to be gravel and large pebbles into pouches, and then packing those away into a duffel bag. The other is making notes in a dirty folder.

He turns the camera 360 degrees to get a full view of the hut.

No one else. Good.

He slips the camera out, disconnects it, and puts it away. He makes tracks to the back of the hut and slips across to check the last one. It's empty, though shows signs of having been ransacked, with clothing and utensils strewn across the floor.

He goes back to the hut with the men. No camouflage, no way to get in stealthily, so he just slips inside the door, moves to its side, and stands with his back to the wall.

* * *

Sideways is still counting when he feels the weight of Zeb's stare and looks up. His face goes slack with astonishment, and then he blurts out, 'Who the fuck are *you*, dude?'

Zeb is impassive. He recognizes Sideways. Conley Stark, thirty-five, ex-Rangers, served twice in Iraq, likes knives, dishonorable discharge for raping a woman.

Stark makes another attempt. *'Qui vous est?'*

Zeb has never believed in pleasantries.

Backside turns around to see what the fuss is about. Brink Schulte, ex-Rangers, served with Conley in Iraq.

'Who the hell is this dumb fuck, Con?'

'Whoever he is, and he's certainly dumb, he'll be dead in a second.'

Zeb remains calm, allowing his presence to fill the room. This will end in only one way.

Stark rises smoothly, and a Gerber Mark II knife appears

in his right hand.

Brink pauses from his bookkeeping to watch Con take out the intruder. He loves a good fight, and Con is the best he has seen with a knife. The bookkeeping can wait for a few minutes.

Or maybe not...

The intruder moves from still to attack in a nanosecond, a silent high leap from a standing position. His left leg takes out Con's knife arm. Brink can hear the bone snap, even as Zeb's right leg collapses Con's throat. *Zero to dead in less than a second*, Brink thinks dimly as the intruder lands smoothly and faces him.

Not even a glance to Con, who is in his death throes.

* * *

Even as Zeb launched his Kalaripayattu strike on Con, he was aware that a third person entered the room, uttered something, grabbed the duffel bag lying near Brink, and made good his escape.

Zeb gazes impassively at Schulte. Answers. Schulte will give them. He has no choice.

An hour later Zeb comes out of the hut.

The Jeep is gone, presumably taken by Holt. It was he who had come into the room during the fight.

Carsten Holt. Unofficial leader of the Rogue Six. *Now Rogue Three*, he corrects himself. Ex-Seal, used by the agency for wet work, expert in close protection work and explosives. Quit the army to go freelance and isn't particular how he earns his money. Now running a mine-hijacking and mineral-trading racket in the Congo. The agency had him on a watch list for some time and had blacklisted him and his closest associates when the Congo happened. The surviving two with Holt are Quink Jones and Pieter Mendes. Both of them ex-Rangers.

He powers up his satellite phone and wakes up Andrews.

Over two hundred women raped – some of them young girls – some children and infants killed. The perpetrators – about forty FDLR soldiers and six ex-agency mercenaries. Many of the villagers in the DRC who worked in the mines had a private stash of ore, which they used to trade, and it was such homes that brought Holt and his band to Luvungi.

The men in the village had been out working in the mines when Holt and the soldiers arrived. Cobalt ore and pebbles were what Stark and Schulte were weighing and recording when Zeb sent them to their Maker. Rape and killing was part of instilling fear and cooperation. Schulte knew that Holt was working with someone in the States for capturing mines and selling the minerals but didn't know who that was.

Andrews goes Chernobyl, his tirade lasting a good few minutes, burning the air. Andrews calms down a long while later.

'You have to come back immediately. We need you to meet the UN and depose. You're the first eyewitness account to this horrific...this atrocious...this sickening...whatever one calls it.'

Zeb is silent.

'I guess Schulte, Stark, and Boulder are in no position to embarrass the agency?' Andrews asks, knowing full well what the answer is.

Zeb keeps his counsel.

'I want you back here immediately. Once the news breaks that FDLR soldiers and some mercenaries who seem to be American were involved in mass murders and multiple rapes in the Congo, the shit will not just hit the fan, it will create a mushroom cloud over Washington. The White House will be brown. I need you back with your photographs and your record of the events to prevent collateral damage here. Your being there, we could spin it that you helped stopped the most horrific abuse in Africa in history. I can see the headlines now.'

Collateral damage.

Andrews-speak for covering his and the Director's ass and playing the D.C. game.

'This's more important than those three. I'll put them on an international blacklist and get international warrants issued on them. In any case, Holt and the other two will likely disappear now that you located them.

'And there's another reason for you to get the hell out of there. The villagers won't be able to distinguish you from the rogue soldiers. Tempers are no doubt going to be high there for some time. I also don't want to explain your presence to the authorities there right now, even if you are listed as a charity worker. You aren't exactly unknown to some intelligence agencies around the world. It's best you get out and come home.'

Zeb looks back at the hut where the girl with the vacant eyes lies, and makes his mind up.

Holt's lifespan can be measured in hours.
He just doesn't know it yet.

Chapter 2

New York – a maelstrom of people and energy. Zeb has spent a day sleeping off his months in the Congo. When he rises after a tabla-playing session, he heats up some soup, opens the windows overlooking 77th Street, and lets the world wash over him.

His second-floor two-bedroom apartment is adequate for his needs. *No, it's too big*, he thinks. Maybe he should downsize further. He looks back towards the tabla resting in the corner of his lounge, the shells dark and gleaming from the streetlights.

He had been walking around in Jamaica, in New York, many years back when he heard the tabla being played in an Indian music school. The taals had stirred something in him that no other instrument had done, something that he thought was dead. He went inside the school and watched a white-haired elderly teacher demonstrate the instrument to a bunch of kids. There were a few drums hanging on the walls of the school. He went closer to view them.

They were strange instruments to him, the curved wooden shell with ropes to tighten the skin, very distinct from Western musical instruments. He ran his palms over the skin of the drums, felt the texture of the black spot, and behind him, he heard the teacher launching into a taal. He lingered around till he heard the students leaving and turned to the teacher.

The teacher was much older than he thought, in his seventies, but still strong of body, bright eyes peering at him through his spectacles. He grasped Zeb's hands without a word and ran his fingers over Zeb's calloused palms, all the while looking into Zeb.

'You will not find forgiveness in the tabla. But you will lose yourself in the drums.'

Zeb started training that day.

Pounding on his door startles him from his reverie.

Andrews. Distinctive and impatient.

'You know the phone was invented for a purpose.' He strides inside, looks around, and finds Zeb's phone on the dining table. 'Twenty calls. Twenty fucking calls and messages from me.'

Zeb shrugs.

'Have you seen the news? Luvungi is front page and has

been on TV all day.'

'I don't follow the news, and I don't have a TV.'

Andrews shakes his head in exasperation. 'Tomorrow is your big day. You're meeting the Secretary-General of the UN, who wants to hear about what happened over there,' he says, waving in the direction of the ocean.

Andrews, being Andrews, is pointing to the wrong ocean. 'The book deals and movie rights will start pouring in now.'

Zeb is amused. 'Is that what you drove through rush-hour traffic to tell me?'

Andrews hesitates, his manic energy subsiding. 'No, I wanted to see you, to see if you were okay. That girl you mentioned...' He trails off and looks searchingly at Zeb.

Zeb ushers him towards the door, saying, 'Pick me up tomorrow,' and shuts the door on Andrews.

He hears Andrews cursing. 'Prick! Why do I bother to be sympathetic? I must need a shrink. You had better be ready at eight sharp tomorrow. I'm not going to take any shit about your waking up late.'

It's cold, crisp, and sunny the next day when Andrews arrives driving an agency car. He's dressed to the nines and drives off without a word as soon as Zeb is seated. Andrews drives with utter disregard for the traffic, honking wildly, sticking his finger out at every opportunity, as he cannons across Roosevelt Avenue and then Queensboro Bridge toward United Nations Plaza.

'Andrews, are you from New York?' Zeb asks.

Andrews flips the bird again as he overtakes a blonde applying lipstick. 'Bronx born and raised. Doesn't it show?'

'Who would have guessed? Hasn't anyone shot at you, the way you drive?' Zeb is unruffled as Andrews overtakes and nearly sideswipes a cab.

'Once this guy chased me all the way from Central Park to Wall Street, waving his handgun. I pulled over and stuck my AK-47 out. He went from Mighty Mouse to Minnie Mouse and drove away.'

Andrews pulls into UN Plaza, the utter professional now. The massacre has made the news, and there's a throng of protestors opposite UN Plaza, many of them holding placards either shaming the UN or urging it to do more. A few news stations have their broadcast vans outside, providing live coverage.

They are whisked upstairs after passing through security, and ushered into a boardroom.

Andrews steps to the window overlooking the plaza and immediately steps back as a few TV cameras train their lenses on him. 'Vultures,' he mutters.

They don't have long to wait. The door opens, and the Secretary-General enters.

'So, Mr. Andrews, we meet again. Never at happy moments, should I say? This is a shameful episode for us,' he says in his dry, precise voice.

He looks at Zeb. 'Major Zebadiah Carter, I have read your file, what little of it Mr. Andrews gave me. I think we owe you thanks for recovering some warheads.'

'I am no longer a major, sir. And I don't know anything about any warheads.'

'Quite. You're the first Western eyewitness to what happened in Luvungi. I want to hear what you saw.'

Zeb recounts without emotion.

The ensuing silence is loud and heavy.

'You're sure about these numbers? No, I take that back; it's a stupid question. The scale of what has happened makes an exact number quite irrelevant.'

'These mercenaries you came across...they were capturing mines and selling the ore to unknown parties? And the FDLR was helping them in this? Or were they helping the FDLR in this?'

'The mercenaries had access to buyers for the ore. They recruited the FDLR to help them hijack the mines,' Zeb replies.

'They told you all this? Just like that?' asks the Secretary-General.

'I did say pretty please,' replies Zeb.

A long pause. 'Quite.

'You could have done more to stop the soldiers,' the official says with the mildest of reproof.

'That's on my head,' Andrews butts in. 'I was the one who asked Zeb not to engage with the soldiers. There were a couple of reasons for that. First, there were about forty of them, and Zeb was alone. He wouldn't be here if he had engaged. Secondly, I had contacted their embassy over here and ours over there to raise hell. Did I do enough? Would Zeb have made a difference? Those questions will haunt me for a long while. I have seen some shit in my life, sir, excuse my language, but this is on a scale that I have never come across.'

'Sir, may I ask a question?' Zeb asks finally, breaking the silence.

The UN official nods.

'Why did you want to meet me? In your position, you will be surrounded by people who can give you the most detailed information; you will have men on the ground or those working with the UN who can give you hourly updates on this. Why me?'

The head of the UN Secretariat smiles humorlessly. 'I wanted to feel what it was like out there.'

On that, his aide steps into the boardroom, signaling the meeting is over. He clasps Zeb's hand in a warm handshake; then they leave.

Andrews is silent as they descend in the elevator.

He is silent as he gets the car on 1st Avenue heading downtown.

'Don't feel guilty. Don't ever feel guilty,' he says suddenly, fiercely, and pounds his horn at a garbage truck, getting the finger in return.

Andrews parks in the basement of a drab-looking building near City Hall.

'The Director wants to meet,' he explains.

Zeb recognizes the building from one of his previous visits as an office frequently used by the agency in New York.

The basement has men in suits at the perimeter, one of them stopping them to see their pass, radioing ahead.

Zeb raises his eyebrows at Andrews, who shrugs and mouths, *I don't know.*

They go up the elevator from the basement to the fourth floor and step into a tightly wound world.

At the elevator they are greeted by another couple of clean-shaven, neatly dressed men who frisk them, check Andrews' identity again, and have whispered conversations in their mics before directing them to a receptionist.

There aren't many people around – the receptionist, a few people hurrying about – but a palpable tension is in the air. He senses Andrews has noticed the charged environment too.

Zeb takes a step back from Andrews, an idea forming in his mind, scans entry and exit corridors, and spots more suits there. The receptionist steps out from behind her desk and leads them to an unmarked meeting room, where the Director awaits. Zeb trails a few steps behind, his senses on full alert.

She regards them calmly, brushes aside Andrews', 'What's burning?' and motions them to sit.

'Andrews has briefed me on the Congo, Zeb. I sent all we know about these military contractors to the FBI and have suggested they get international arrest warrants issued. I should hear from them shortly. I have also asked them to put an alert out on all incoming and outgoing flights. It's possible the remaining three will return to the US. Andrews, will you...'

She stops as an inner concealed door opens and the President of the United States enters.

Chapter 3

Zeb rises instinctively, Andrews doing the same with his jaw dropping open. The Director clears her throat, breaking the spell over Andrews.

The President says, 'Clare, I'm sorry for interrupting. I wanted a word with you on that dossier before heading off to Washington. Sorry, guys, I have to kidnap your boss for a moment.'

The Director says, 'Sir, this is Andrews, my right-hand man, and this is Major Zebadiah Carter. I have mentioned the Congo to you. Zeb was there.'

The President sizes up both of them. 'Andrews, Major, there are many of you who work unsung and unheard in protecting our country and often safeguarding global security. Some of you work within the remit of the government and' – he focuses on Zeb – 'some outside.'

He looks old and weary as he addresses Zeb. 'Major, we have let down that part of the world badly. I'm glad that you were there to raise the first alert, though Clare tells me that you did quite a bit more than that – that you have done things I'm not supposed to know about. Know this, that I am very grateful for the work of people like you and Andrews.'

The Director suggests they meet later and dismisses them.

Andrews is still a little dazed as they head back towards his car. 'The Secretary-General and the President in one day. Andrews, my boy, you can die happy now,' he mutters.

Andrews drops him off on Broadway with a promise to update him on progress with the FBI.

Zeb tells him finding Holt's conduit in the US is the key to finding Holt.

Zeb strolls along Broadway, soaking in the energy, buys soup from a vendor in Times Square, and walks towards Central Park. New York is as much a jungle as the Congo is. The rules aren't that different. The predators aren't that different. Zeb is good at hunting predators in jungles, wherever the jungle is.

Noise drops off in the verdant expanse of the park as Zeb walks along West Drive and reaches Springbanks Arch. He finds a bench near the arch, slows his metabolism, and becomes one with time.

* * *

She comes when its pitch black, when even the foolhardy

would never enter the park alone. She has attempted to take her life on a couple of occasions but lost her nerve at the last minute. She has now come to die in the park, in its most remote section, hoping the darkness and her misery will help her take her own life.

She finds a bench in the darkest part of the park near Springbanks Arch, rummages through the bag she has brought, and removes a sharp kitchen knife. She pulls up the sleeves of her sweater and turns her left wrist upward. She's not sure how she should do this and takes a deep breath before placing the knife over her wrist.

'That's a messy way to die, and there's no guarantee it will work,' a voice calls out from the dark.

She starts, and the knife slips from her hand. She gropes for it in the dark while looking around. Nothing, just the dark and the shadows.

'You can't stop me. I'll cut myself before you reach me,' she calls out defiantly, no fear in her voice. She is past fear.

A chuckle. 'I've never stopped anyone from dying. In fact, I've helped many toward that very end.'

'Are you going to leave?' she asks.

'No.'

'Who are you? Why can't you leave me alone?'

'I was sitting here alone and at peace when you arrived, interrupting my serenity, and now you wish to create problems for me.'

'What problems did I create for you? I didn't even know you were here.'

'If you kill yourself, I have to carry your body to the hospital, talk to the police, and fill out forms...so much hassle. You're a heavy person, so carrying you won't be easy either.'

His tone is dispassionate, not mocking, yet she is angered.

'I guess it's all a joke to you, huh? I bet you don't have the slightest clue what acute depression feels like. When you lie on the bed and the room closes in on you, the world closes in on you, you suffocate. When there's nothing to look forward to when you wake up. Your friends, family, and colleagues give up on you because they see you as a lost cause. Death is the only exit.'

A very long pause. She's not sure if he's still there or gone. The park has gone silent as if listening to them.

Then, 'I know what it feels like. I have been there. I live it every day.'

She barks out a laugh. 'Right! Next you'll be telling me you suffer from acute depression too. Dude, I tried taking my life twice before. If you felt as bad as I do, you wouldn't be around.'

'I have never wanted to take the easy way. Taking my life would be easy. I don't want to make it easy on myself.'

She casts her eyes around, trying to find him, but can't see anything other than layered shadows. She sits a long while, reflecting on the weird conversation. She calls out a few times but receives no reply. She's now not even sure whether there was anyone there or whether it was just voices in her head. The adrenaline in her body seeps away, replaced by the chill-to-the-bone damp night air. She stands sluggishly, packs the knife back in the bag, and makes her way to 100th Street.

* * *

Zeb watches her leave the park and pursues her at a distance. At this time of night there is still traffic, a few pedestrians out and about, and he's able to blend in. This is New York, after all.

He follows her down the subway entrance and watches her board a train from a hundred yards away.

He catches the down train and goes home.

He lies in bed thinking for a long time of vacant eyes, of what makes people take their own lives.

It's time to start hunting tomorrow.

He calls Broker the next day.

Broker is just that. He served with military intelligence and was injured during his time in Mogadishu. After receiving an honorable discharge from the army, he went back to college, got a degree in Information Systems from Syracuse University, discovered hacking, and lived the corporate life a few years.

Finding it too staid, he went into doing what he was best at. Sourcing information.

Outside the army, he discovered a knack for entrepreneurship and developed a reputable business out of selling information: information on African dictators, the sexual habits of US senators, security practices of oil companies, buying habits of East European crime gangs, weapons systems, reams of pages on military contractors – anything he could turn a profit from. Most of his clients were national governments, intelligence agencies around the world, defense contractors, international corporations, and security firms.

He and Zeb went back a long way. Zeb was the reason he still had his right leg. He walked with a slight limp, but that beat a prosthetic any day.

Zeb gets Broker's voice mail.

'Message. Number. You know the drill,' his baritone rumbles through the phone.

Zeb hangs up without leaving a message.

He calls Andrews, gets his voice mail, too. Andrews' voice mail greeting is a recitation of the Miranda rights. Funny.

He prints the photographs from his phone, writes up his report, and emails it to Andrews. With nothing else to do, it's time to attend to family. He spruces up and catches the subway to Manhattan, changes at Times Square, and goes to Hamilton Heights.

His destination is a mid-rise west of Broadway. The doorman knows him well and ushers him to the elevator. The apartment is empty when he lets himself in. He makes himself a cup of coffee and settles down to wait in the living room.

He is on the Basanti Bukhari raga on the tabla in his mind when, a couple of hours later, a key scrapes at the door. The door is flung open by a seven-year-old boy, who marches to the kitchen, opens the fridge, and helps himself to a can of fruit juice.

He returns to the living room and finally spots Zeb sitting motionless.

Blue eyes widen in astonishment as they regard Zeb.

'Who are you? What're you doing here?' The words spill out angrily.

Full-on New York accent, healthy complexion, spends a lot of time outdoors, black hair, blue eyes, just returned from school, still in his uniform, satchel slung over his shoulders; all this Zeb notes without conscious thought.

'How did you get in? Did you break into Nana's house?'

No fear, notes Zeb. Most boys his age would be panicking.

'I know. You've come to steal Nana's money, haven't you?' He darts into the kitchen and comes out with a kitchen knife. 'Don't come near me, and don't move. I'm gonna call my mom.'

With that, he runs out of the apartment and locks it behind him. Zeb hears rushing feet outside the door minutes later, whispers, and the door opens. The boy stomps in followed by a blonde who is obviously his mother. The blue eyes and features come from her.

She's flustered and says sheepishly, 'You're Zeb, right? Cassandra's brother? Sorry about Rory. He gets a little overprotective.' She nudges Rory. 'Actually, you're the one who should say sorry.'

'Why should I apologize for looking out for Nana? I didn't know who he was. He didn't say a single word to me when I asked him. Even now he's not exactly talkative, is he?'

The blonde turns to Zeb and introduces herself, 'I'm Lauren Balthazar, and this little ball of goodwill and cheerfulness is my son, Rory. We're Cassandra's neighbors – as of a few months ago. Cassandra's at work at City College, but she should be back in a couple of hours.'

She observes him as she's talking: tall, about six feet, brown hair, serious, lean and unnaturally still. And he still hasn't uttered a word. She thinks Rory was right to freak out at Zeb's silence.

She relieves Rory of the carving knife and puts it back where it belongs. On returning to the living room, she asks, 'Want some coffee? Or lunch? It's no trouble.' *And it's the least I can do after my son pulled a knife on you.*

Zeb shakes his head.

She pauses, uncertain. 'All right, then. We'll be right next door if you need anything.'

Rory is still glaring at Zeb as she drags him away. Stillness returns, and Zeb resumes Basanti Bukhari and waits. He's good at waiting.

* * *

It's evening when Cassandra enters the apartment. 'Hi, Zeb! Lauren called me, but I was caught up with some students after classes. Sorry to have kept you waiting.'

She goes to her bedroom to change and calls out from there. 'Lauren has invited us to dinner. Hope you can stay.'

She goes to the kitchen and, in a few minutes, returns with two steaming cups of coffee.

Placing his in front of him, she sits across from him and studies him. He hasn't changed much. A few more wrinkles around his eyes, some grey in his hair. 'How have you been? Clare told me you were out of the country. When did you get back?'

Clare, the Director.

Cassandra and Clare had been to Bryn Mawr together, and then later on to Penn. Clare had started working at the agency as an analyst and was the first female director of the agency. Cassandra had started her career as a foreign service specialist in the State Department, was noticed, and became the aide to the Secretary of State. Clare's and Cassandra's friendship had weathered the politics of Washington, and they frequently bounced ideas off each other. After a time, Washington had palled for Cassandra, whereupon she quit to pursue an academic career in New York. If anything, the Director and Zeb's sister had gotten closer now that she had left Washington.

'A couple of days ago,' he replies.

'And how have you been?'

He shrugs. Talking, feelings, that was never his thing.

She sits for a long time, watching him. She is so much older than he, yet thinks he has seen and experienced much more than she ever will. People who don't know him mistake his self-containment for loneliness. 'Okay. I should know better than to even ask. I'm going to get dressed for dinner at Lauren's.' She shrugs mentally. He has always been a mystery. Nothing new there.

She slides a key across. 'I keep them in the sideboard.'

He opens the sideboard and removes a pair of tablas. These were gifted to him by his guru in Jamaica. Since his first visit to the school, he'd spent hours learning the tabla, the various taals, and had often accompanied his guru in his performances. His guru had been right. He hadn't found what he was seeking in tabla, but the drums provided an escape.

He takes out a soft cloth and polishes the wooden shell of the sidda and then repeats the polishing on the brass of the dagga. He adjusts the tension ropes on the sides of the drums and cleans them carefully. He takes a basalt stone and polishes the black spots, the syahi, on the drums slowly and rhythmically.

Cass observes from her bedroom. She doesn't understand his fascination for Indian drums. As a child, he wasn't musically inclined. Zeb puts away the drums when she emerges ten minutes later, dressed to the nines, and they make their way to the apartment next door.

Rory opens the door with a flourish. 'Hello, Aunt Cassie, I helped Mom make dinner for us, so I bet you it'll be good.'

'You've trained me well, Rory. I would never dare say your dinner is bad,' Cass replies. 'You have met Zeb, haven't you?' she asks with a mirthful glint in her eye.

Rory squirms and shuffles and then sticks his chin out. 'He shouldn't have let himself in, Aunt Cassie. I could have called the cops, and then it would have been a bigger scene.'

Lauren comes along with a tall dark-haired man. 'Rory, shush. We all know how well you watch over Cassie's apartment. Zeb, this is my husband, Connor. Connor, this is Zeb, Cassie's brother.'

The man has a firm grip as he shakes Zeb's hand.

Connor is an award-winning journalist working at the *New York Times*. He started his career at local newspapers in Kentucky and became noticed nationally when he exposed corruption in southeastern Kentucky politics. His big break came when he was snapped up by the *New York Post*. He trained his sights on exposing the corrupt practices of New York's senators, won a George Polk award for that story, and moved to the *New York Times*, where he took on global features.

He opens a bottle of wine and makes small talk as they sit around the living room. Lauren says she's expecting Connor's sister for dinner, as well. She works in an advertising agency and is nearly always late for any occasion.

His sister enters just as Lauren finishes her apologies. Anne Balthazar is as tall as Connor, maybe five eleven, athletic build, and with the same dark hair, blue eyes and healthy complexion.

Rory jumps up with a squeal and flings himself into her arms. He rips at the paper on the gift she has brought him and squeals even louder when he finds a pair of baseball batting gloves in the box.

Connor asks Zeb about his work. Zeb shrugs and says he does investigative work for the army occasionally and some security consulting work for businesses.

Connor has done his own investigating on Cassandra and her family. It has become a force of habit to do a lookup on whoever he meets. He knows from his sources at the agency and at other agencies that Zeb is held in high regard and has worked on several consulting assignments which he knows is agency-speak for covert, deniable assignments.

Over dinner, Rory asks him, 'Uncle Zeb, have you been in any war?'

'Just Zeb,' Zeb replies. 'A few.'

'Must have been fun. Did you kill a lot of enemies?'

Anne reprimands him. 'Wars are never fun, Rory. They're horrible and cause death and destruction.

'What?' she says on seeing Zeb's slight smile. 'I guess you don't agree. Wait, I forgot. You make your living from wars, don't you?'

Zeb shakes his head. 'Wars are destructive and horrible. I don't disagree.' He says nothing more.

Anne is disappointed that he's ducking out of a debate, but doesn't pursue it.

Rory, his Xbox war games instincts aroused, doesn't give up. 'Well, Zeb, if you didn't like war, you'd have quit being a soldier, right? Aunt Cassie says you're rolling in dough, so it's not as if you need to work.'

The noise drops, and all eyes swivel to Zeb.

'War isn't only about killing or destroying. It can be about protecting and defending, too.'

'That's bullshit,' Anne retorts, and Rory covers his ears and grimaces comically. 'Sorry, honey. But, Zeb, most countries go to war out of greed and politics. Very few wars have happened because the aggressor country had to defend itself.'

'You may be right, ma'am. I'm just a paid grunt and follow orders.'

'Oh, you can do better than that! Maybe you do like war,' she exclaims.

'It pays my wages, ma'am,' replies Zeb, with the slightest trace of a smile.

She's not sure if he's genuinely avoiding an argument or pulling her leg. Lauren interrupts their conversation by serving Rory's favorite dessert, chocolate cake, knocking Rory out of the conversation and into many minutes of ecstatic eating. Later they adjourn to the living room, and over coffee, Connor asks Zeb if he has heard of Senator Rob Hardinger.

Zeb shrugs. 'Nope, but then I've been out of the country and haven't been tracking politics.'

'Hardinger is a key party fund-raiser, has proximity to

the President because of his fund-raising activities, yet is scum. His family business, Alchemy Holdings, is into mining and minerals trading. It's an old, established business, held privately, that was started by the Senator's grandfather. The business has mines in Australia, Central and South America, and Africa. They mine and trade diamonds, aluminum, copper, tin, you name it.'

Zeb keeps silent, not sure where this is going.

Connor takes a long sip of his coffee. 'I got interested in them when I was looking into corporate lobbying and heard rumors about Alchemy Holdings making party donations to influence government policy. Now lobbying is a standard practice and so is making corporate donations – nothing illegal there. However, the whispers are that Alchemy paid off senators and congressmen *directly* to change policy and to remove trade restrictions with certain countries on certain items.'

'I have also been looking into Alchemy's ethical practices at the mines they own in South America and Africa. I have reason to believe the work practices are exploitative.'

Zeb shrugs. 'I don't see what's so new or earthshaking about this. Big businesses have been lobbying politicians since time and politics began, and business practices in South America and Africa aren't the same as ours. They've always exploited their workers.'

Connor smiles devilishly. 'Yes, I agree on both counts, but what Alchemy did wasn't lobbying. It was bribing. And what if I said there was a provable trail that showed Hardinger sanctioned the payoffs and the exploitative practices when he was the Chairman and CEO of Alchemy?'

Anne pipes up, 'Wouldn't he have to resign the Senate and face charges, possibly criminal, if this were provable?'

'That's what I'm working on currently.' Connor leans back contentedly. He eyes Zeb and asks, 'I'm visiting Africa next week to investigate Alchemy's mines and the mining conditions of Western-owned mines in general. You were in Africa for some time, weren't you? Did you come across any American-owned mines or hear of the working conditions there?'

Zeb smiles. 'I was just a grunt taking orders, doing routine army stuff over there. I didn't pay any attention to anything but those orders.'

Anne is struck by how young and carefree he looks when he smiles.

It's late when they break up. Connor wants to meet him when he's back from Africa and get his views on his findings.

Cassandra asks Zeb to stay with her for a few days; he is her only family. He keeps a set of clothes at her apartment for such occasions. He checks his phone when alone and notices voice mails from Broker and Andrews. He sends a text to Broker suggesting they meet tomorrow.

'This Hardinger story is creating some tension between Lauren and Connor. Connor has received threats if he doesn't drop his story on Alchemy,' says Cassandra, joining him in the living room. 'Connor is too credible a journalist to buckle under such pressure, plus it's not like he hasn't been threatened before. But Lauren's worried – it feels different to her because Hardinger's a high-profile public figure.'

'He's been anxious to meet you ever since I told him you were in the Special Forces. Maybe I shouldn't have mentioned that.' She looks at him apologetically.

He shrugs; it's done. He's not particularly interested in Connor's story unless it intersects with his hunt for Holt.

The chances of that happening are pretty remote.

Chapter 4

The next day, Cass hands him a note as she leaves. 'You. Me. Baseball. Evening.'

She says Rory slipped it under the apartment door on his way to school, after learning that Zeb was staying for a few days.

'Why has he given this to me? Doesn't he have other friends to play with, or doesn't Connor play with him?'

'He has a friend or two, but he doesn't make friends easily – and he likes you. What's wrong with that? In his seven years, the boy has seen constant relocation, moving from Kentucky to New York, and within New York a few more times. All this has led to problems with making friends.

'As for Connor and Lauren,' Cass continues, 'they're busy in their careers. He can be a bit demanding. It's okay to say no to him.'

Zeb says he'll think about it. He isn't sure whether he'll have time to spend with Rory and whether he wants to. To add to that, he doesn't intend to stay more than two or three more days at Cassandra's.

He wipes it from his mind and goes to meet Broker.

Meeting Broker requires counter-surveillance tactics. There are many who would love to grab hold of Broker and extract his information. Zeb spends a few hours in the subway randomly changing trains, walking aimlessly over ground, going through large stores; the idea is to lose any tails or make them die of boredom.

He enters a bar on Allen Street and spots Broker immediately, holding court at his table with a few others roaring at his jokes. Broker is the soul of any party. He's tall, blond, great looking, in great shape, and always stylishly dressed; his ready wit, rich voice and a barely discernible limp draw people to him. It also helps that he always picks up the check.

He shoos away his admirers on spotting Zeb and gives him a long hug when Zeb bends down to greet him. They catch up on old times for a while, discussing friends past and lost.

Zeb gives him the dossiers of Holt, Mendes, and Jones. 'I'm hunting these three. These are agency dossiers. They may be in the US, they may be abroad. I want to know who they work with, who's employed them, where they're based.'

Broker fingers them without opening them. 'Why isn't the agency helping you on this?'

'They're also looking into it. Rather, they've asked the FBI to dig up those details.'

'Then they'll get dick. Those assholes will run circles round them all the while giving them the polite face.' Broker's respectful opinion on one of the world's foremost investigative agencies. He drums his fingers on the folders. 'Is this related to the Congo?'

Zeb isn't surprised that Broker knew where he'd been, even though this was one assignment Zeb hadn't mentioned to him. Broker's gotten to where he is because he has an intelligence network that rivals the agency's, pays well for information, and has tight lips. Zeb gives him the background as Broker continues drumming his fingers. Broker has seen enough shit to last him a lifetime. He has his own code. No women. No children. Nothing against the national interest. He is very choosy about his clients and likes to know why they want a particular piece of information. If in doubt, he informally runs his assignments, before taking them on, past certain federal agencies. Like a credit check.

'They might still be in Africa, or they might be here. We want to find them and also find out who their conduit is,' Zeb finishes.

Broker looks at him, brows furrowed. 'The kind of work you get involved in – terrorists, lost weapons, security consulting – this doesn't sound like something the agency should be losing a lot of sleep over or for them to involve you in. It's not their problem, really. I don't buy the bullshit Andrews fed you.'

Zeb shrugs. 'I am involved. I don't care about the agency's motives.'

'Okay. I'll see what I can get for you. I'm as interested in getting these guys as you are. They give us warriors a bad name.'

He heads off to the bar to pay the tab, but the bartender waves him away, refusing to take his money. It's on the house since Broker entertained so many of the patrons and was good for business. Typical Broker. Goes on a business visit and gets the frills paid for.

They part ways outside the bar to start their elaborate counter-surveillance routine. 'Hey, Zeb,' Broker calls him back. 'Damn, nearly forgot. This is for you.' He hands over a leather case.

Zeb opens the expensive leather case and removes a pair of wraparound Aviator sunglasses. He tries them on; they fit perfectly. 'I like them, but I have enough of these.'

Broker chortles. 'You've never seen a pair like these, my friend. They're the latest in counter-surveillance toys. They have tiny cameras fitted at the rear of the frames, and those cameras project on the corner of the lenses. The cameras focus the images automatically for the eyes, so that the eyes can see those normally. There's a tiny switch near the right lens which turns the cameras on or off. The batteries go on for years. The NSA uses these, but I improved them. I installed another switch on the left – you can now forward the images to an email address or to another server.'

'There are only two pairs of these sunglasses. I have one, and you have the other. Try to take care of them. Repairs are a bitch.'

And with that, Broker is off.

Zeb tries the glasses and the cameras and finds that they work perfectly. With some practice, turning them off and on becomes a casual gesture. He's getting addicted to these gizmos that Broker supplies.

He executes his elaborate counter-surveillance routine, this time with the Aviators to help, and reaches Cassandra's apartment a few hours later.

Rory is waiting impatiently for him with his baseball glove and school bag. He looks up with a frown as Zeb enters the apartment. 'Dude, I bet you don't keep your girlfriends waiting. Let's go now. It's not long before dark.'

He goes to the door and looks back at Zeb. 'You heard me, didn't you, dude?'

Zeb, his life hijacked, follows him down the apartment block and a walk across another block. Rory takes them to Riverbank State Park, where he dons his baseball glove. They spend a couple of hours pitching and catching. Rory has excellent hand-eye coordination and catches most of Zeb's pitches.

Rory flops on the turf after practice, lies back and stares at the sky. He looks at Zeb, who is lying still beside him. 'Does anything scare you, Zeb?'

Zeb looks at him and shakes his head.

Rory's lips tremble. 'My mom and dad fight almost every day. Mom keeps telling Dad that his work is too dangerous. I know some kids whose Moms and Dads don't live with each other anymore, and I don't want to be like them.'

He sniffs, wipes a tear, takes out some books from his school bag and does his homework. Seven years old, the weight of the world on his shoulders, and he has the presence of mind to do his homework in a park on a sunny New York evening.

Lauren spots them from her bedroom window as they approach the mid-rise entrance. She hasn't been able to figure Zeb out; none of them have been able to. She's not sure a loner, a self-contained person like Zeb is the right company for Rory. As they come closer, she observes Rory skipping and smothers her protective instincts. *Do nothing for now*, she thinks.

Andrews hasn't much to tell Zeb when he calls him. The FBI will come back to Andrews when they have something – exactly like Broker said it would pan out.

The next day, he decides to check out Holt's last known address, Jackson, New Jersey, home to Six Flags Great Adventure and about an hour away from New York. He knows it's probably a long shot, but he's already weary of inaction. He leaves a message for Cassie that he's going out and heads for the nearest Enterprise to rent a car.

An hour later he's in a Cherokee on I-78, heading toward New Jersey via Garden State Parkway. With the wind in his hair, his Glock, knife, and ankle gun with him, Zeb is ready. He reaches Jackson close to noon and checks out the town by first stopping for a bite at the Jackson Diner. With its retro look, the diner is representative of many such small towns, where time goes slower and the world is confined to the neighborhood.

After lunch, he tours the town, searching for realtors, and chooses a smaller one.

Zeb poses as an investor from New York looking to get away from the big, bad city. He has his cover complete with business cards, a fancy title at a venture capital firm in Manhattan and pictures of a happy, smiling family. Any calls to the firm will get routed to Broker or Andrews. Zeb has many such covers.

The realtor is too happy to help Zeb. Business is slow, 'For Sale' signs dot the town, and homes are not moving.

The realtor drives him across the township spread across a hundred miles. It's a nice oasis away from New York. They spend a couple of hours looking at a few choice properties within Zeb's budget.

Zeb asks him to drive past Chesterfield Drive. The agent looks at him, a question in his eyes. Zeb shrugs and says some of his friends were looking at houses there, so he wanted to see the area.

Chesterfield Drive is not far from I-95 at one end, and the Metedeconk Golf Club is close by the other. Zeb spots Holt's house easily. It's a single-family home and is the only house that appears deserted. The windows are bare, newspapers piled on the porch.

The realtor notices Zeb's glance. 'It's been deserted for a long time. Family home owned by some guy in the army who hardly comes back to it. No one else stays there. I left a note a year or so back, to see if he wanted to sell. Didn't hear a peep out of him.' Shakes his head at the injustice of a world unwilling to help him sell a house.

Zeb ignores him. He notes the single garage, the spacing between the house and its neighbors, possible entry and exit points. They come to the end of the road and turn onto Colchester Drive and head back. More viewings, more monologues from the realtor, and they're done for the day. Zeb pays him the earnest money, promises to be back next week for a second viewing on a house, and makes his escape to his Cherokee.

Zeb enters Chesterfield Drive again and parks his vehicle a few houses away. He walks to Holt's house, as if seeking directions, and rings the bell. He waits a while and then walks around the house, peering through the windows.

Through the kitchen windows at the back, he can make out thick layers of dust on the sink and kitchen counter. He circles the house fully, but there's no sign that anyone's been there recently.

He goes back to the Cherokee and prepares to drive away, but turns the engine off as a thought strikes him.

He walks back to the house and slips a note under the door. It's a simple message – '*I am coming.*'

On the way back, he calls Broker. Broker tells him that Holt and the other two are definitely back in the USA. 'They flew out of the Congo the second day after you left, under assumed identities. I have their biometrics coming in at JFK. I have put an alert on their debit and credit cards, and have put the word out in my network. Let's see what bites.'

Broker hears silence from Zeb's end, just the muted sounds of traffic. Then, 'Pass the word to your network that I'm hunting them. Let them know I'm coming.'

'Why? That will alert them, won't it? Oh, I get it. You want them to be always looking over their shoulder. Dude, I like your style.'

He calls Broker again as he nears Hamilton Heights.

'Two calls in one day? If you don't watch out, you'll use up your conversation quota for the whole year.'

'Senator Hardinger,' Zeb says.

'What about him?'

'His family company has mining interests in Africa and South America. Who manages them? Who all are employed there?'

'That's a different shark you're going after, Zeb. You think there's a connection? A little far-fetched, don'tcha think?'

Silence.

'Right. I'll dig into his background and let you know. Give me a few.'

Zeb reaches Cassandra's apartment late in the evening and finds Rory playing on his PSP.

'Aunt Cassie said you went out. I was hoping to get in some baseball practice. Will you be staying a few days, Zeb?'

Zeb shakes his head. 'No, I have to go back to my apartment tonight.'

Rory's face falls, but he doesn't say anything.

'Next time I come, maybe we can go camping.'

Rory lets out a shrill whoop, pumps his fist, and zips out of the room to tell his mom.

Cassandra looks at Zeb. 'Do you have any idea what you're getting into?'

Zeb smiles his rare smile. 'Not really, but when has that stopped me? I need to go back to my apartment.'

'I think Connor will want to meet you when he's back from Africa. I'll call you when he's home.'

The subway carries him back to Jackson Heights, tubes full of people moving from light to dark and then light.

Chapter 5

A ndrews pays him a visit a week later. They meet at a bar in downtown Manhattan, Andrews looking tired and disheveled.

'I don't have good news for you. I've been asked to back off by the FBI.'

Silence fills the space.

'Holt is doing a deal with those bastards. In return for immunity, he's offering a mother lode, their words, of information on Al Qaeda recruitment in the Congo.'

Zeb sits immobile, watching Andrews.

'He contacted them as soon as he returned from Africa. He said he had vital intel on Al Qaeda in Africa.

'Terrorism, Al Qaeda, those are the magic budget words, Zeb. Try to understand. The Feds have given him immunity in return for whatever information he can give them. What threatens our country is more important than what happened over there.'

Zeb walks away without a word.

'You know backing off applies to you too,' Andrews calls at Zeb's back.

He walks a long time, seeing nothing and hearing nothing. The rage makes the city disappear, the landscape barren and shrouded in dark.

He emerges from his dark fog a few hours later to find himself sitting on his favorite bench in Central Park, near Springbanks Arch. He wonders briefly which other lost souls have sat there in the interim.

As he makes his way back to his apartment, he's surprised at his reaction to the whole deal. He should have expected something like this would happen. After all, Andrews and the Director lived in a political world.

But nothing has changed for him, and with that, he takes out his tabla and plays into the night.

A few days later, Broker calls. He hasn't been able to get much more on Holt or his conduit. Holt seems to have dropped off the grid even though he's sharing intel with the FBI. Broker's network has someone who is happy to talk with Zeb, though.

'Kelly is damaged goods. He left the forces a few years back, couldn't get over the PTSD after his four stints in Afghanistan.

He fed me some good intel, and when he heard I was looking for Holt, he contacted me. He refuses to tell me what he has and will only talk to you. He doesn't know anything about you, just says he wants to talk to my client directly.'

Broker continues, 'This could be a setup.'

Zeb thinks about it for a moment. 'Set up the meet – in the same bar we met, on Allen Street.'

'Will do. I'll get back to you when it's set.'

Two days later, Zeb meets Kelly.

Broker offered to watch his back, but Zeb works best alone. Zeb arrives a few hours early, driving a ubiquitous yellow cab, having paid the cab driver to take the day off, and parks away from the bar, with a good view of the entrance. He doesn't see any surveillance. He has been wearing Broker's fancy shades, and those haven't revealed any tails either.

He sees Kelly entering the bar alone and on time. He waits another half hour and walks down an entire block, either side of the bar, casually. Nothing and no one stands out.

Kelly is nursing a drink alone when Zeb walks to the bar and orders one for himself.

Kelly is grizzled, in his forties and looks like a veteran, with his well-kept body and close-cropped hair. He looks up as Zeb takes a stool, his eyes sharp. 'Broker sent you?'

Zeb nods. They size each other up for a long moment, and then Kelly downs his drink in a large gulp and signals for another.

'Holt? You looking to hire him? Or looking for him?'

Zeb doesn't reply.

Kelly waits a moment. 'You don't talk much, do you? Broker did mention that. I'm dying. Liver. Too much to drink. Not many months left now, so when I heard Broker was looking for the lowdown on Holt, I got in touch. Call it conscience or guilt. Whatever you want.

'Holt and I were in 'Stan together.' Afghanistan, 'Stan to those who'd served there. 'Many years and many bodies back. He was our commander. We were deployed at FOB Sharana. We lost so many men there. Not a day passed when we didn't have a rocket attack, an IED explosion, snipers...everything that was devised to kill American soldiers was deployed there.

'This was in the days when fighting with the Taliban was at its peak and parlaying with the locals wasn't done. We spent the days patrolling and the nights afraid to sleep. Over a period of time, a strange bond developed between him and me. I did a lot of scouting, and he relied on my intel. He had excellent tactical skills, lacked an emotional core, but I knew – we all knew – if anyone could get most of us out of Sharana alive, it was him.

'We didn't like each other, but he respected my abilities, and I respected his.

'Very often he and I patrolled together, and it was in the second year that we started patrolling a small village far from our base. There was nothing there; to call it a village was being generous. Maybe not more than thirty people lived there, goat herders and their women and children in a few huts.

'Holt used to disappear into that village and asked me to keep guard and patrol outside it. I didn't give much thought to this, since I figured he was just being friendly with the locals and getting information.

'During the day, the men used to take their goats away for grazing, leaving the women and children behind. One day it took him too long to recon, so I went into the village to look for him. Everything seemed normal, some women cooking, a few kids playing around. Those huts were basic, just mud walls, a roof and a hole for a door and another hole for a window.

'Holt emerged from the last hut as I was approaching it, and blew his stack when he spotted me. He screamed at me for leaving my patrol and putting us at risk. I was only half listening, because through the hole in the hut I could see a woman getting dressed. I realized what Holt had been up to.

'Back at the unit I talked with the others. It turned out they knew. But they suspected he was raping the women. All the women in that village.'

Kelly takes a long pull of his drink. His thousand-yard stare looks out at the bar but sees the hills and brush of Sharana.

'Those were different days. The political climate was different. They were the enemy, and we had to kill them. No one said a word to Holt because he was our commander.

'A month later we had a sniper attack. Sumbitch took out three of our men. Holt went into a rage. He increased the patrols, triangulated the sniper's location and tried to track him. But it's a huge country, and those sumbitches just become invisible.

'In the evening, Holt went to the village, rounded up two women and shot them. Just like that. Not a word said, nothing.

Grabbed them by the arm, took them to a wall, and shot them. And as if that wasn't enough, he shot a kid, maybe five, six years old. Bam, bam, bam. Over.

'He then turned his gun on some of the men approaching him; they fell back. And he trained his gun on me.

'This all happened in less than a minute. My brain was still processing it all when I see this gun barrel on me.

'He finally lowered it and walked away. Not a word was said at camp the next few days. A rumor spread that the village was sheltering that sniper and they had to be taught a lesson.

'We were raw guys, eighteen, nineteen years old. Green to the gills and shit scared. We didn't have the balls to complain to the higher-ups about Holt. I left 'Stan a few months later. I heard Holt had moved around a bit, but slowly lost track of him. Guilt ate away at me the initial few years, and then I started rationalizing the events, and then time did its thing.

'To this day, I have no idea how he thought, what motivated him. He was an unpredictable sumbitch.' He wags his finger in Zeb's face. 'Remember that. Unpredictable. That's what makes him dangerous. Assuming you're hunting him.'

Sounds of the bar fill the silence.

'I don't know much about him. He wasn't very open about himself. I know he had a mother somewhere in Jersey, and he mentioned her more than a couple of times. That's all that I can give you. I don't know if this helps you, but it helps me.'

'Are you sure about the mother?' asks Zeb.

'Hell, this was some years back, and my memory isn't what it was. But yes, he did mention a mother in Jersey.'

Zeb doesn't remember any kin mentioned in Holt's dossier. This could be something Broker and he could use.

'Do me a favor,' he tells Kelly, 'spread the word that I'm hunting Holt.'

Kelly smiles grimly and nods.

He settles the tab and watches Kelly amble away. 'Stan had a lot to answer for.

He goes back to his dossiers when he is back at his apartment. Nope. No mother listed for Holt. No kin at all. He calls Broker and briefs him on the meeting. Broker says Holt doesn't have any siblings, not on record anyway, and his father passed away a while back. That's in the dossier. So his mother is the only surviving kin.

Broker says he'll get a list of Holts living in New Jersey who are fifty years old and above, since that will be approximately the age range for Holt's mother . Broker has access to Social Security and DMV databases. Zeb doesn't know if he hacks into them or has access to them through his network.

Broker calls back in the evening with two hundred names and addresses fitting the approximate age profile for Holt's mother in New Jersey.

The next day Zeb starts calling each of those addresses. He is calling on behalf of the Department of Defense to inform them of increased pension benefits to the next of kin of veterans. That's his cover. It never hurts to appeal to greed.

After three hours of calling, he is just two-thirds down the list. So far none of the Holts are the one he's looking for. Several of those Holts have kin in the armed forces, but none of them are Carsten Holt or anyone resembling him.

He takes a break, strips down to loose, flowing trousers, and does his deep-breathing exercises. His living room is spacious, and its wooden flooring and high roof make it a good dojo-at-home.

Once he completes his breathing exercises, he starts off with simple Kalaripayattu moves, progressing to more complex; his body seamlessly blends motion and stillness. Kalaripayattu is one of the oldest martial arts in the world and has its roots in the tiny state of Kerala in India. Zeb had been lucky to be taken under the wing of a seventy-year-old gurukkal, a teacher.

Zeb showers after his training and gets back to his calling. It's dusk by the time he has gone through all the names. He has had to go back and call a few of the names again since he didn't get a person the first time he called. There are still about thirty names for whom he left voice mails.

He opens a can of soup, warms it up, and eats it with garlic bread as he watches the city prepare itself for another night.

He checks his phone later and finds a message from Cassandra. Connor is back from Africa and wants to meet with him. So does Rory.

The next day, Zeb calls the remaining addresses, reaches most of them, has no luck with them, and leaves a voice mail for the remaining.

He calls Broker to ask him if he has any update on Hardinger. Broker tells him he's putting together a dossier and should be ready in a few days.

Zeb heads out to Cassandra's, and when he nears her mid-rise, he spots them. One of them is across the street reading a newspaper and seemingly casual but observing the entrance. The other has taken a leaf from Zeb's book; he is slumped in the driver's seat in a yellow cab, off-duty sign on, parked just short of the building. He's wearing shades and holding a book in front of him, but Zeb can see that he's also observing the entrance.

They haven't spotted him, if he is the one they are watching for. Zeb gets a cappuccino from a café and watches them. The one on the street is checking out anyone approaching the mid-rise, and the one in the cab is watching the forecourt of the mid-rise. They are wearing throat microphones and tiny colorless earpieces. The one on the street occasionally looks at the cabbie as they speak.

After nearly an hour of study, Zeb decides to force their hands. He crosses the street in plain view of both and approaches the entrance of the building from the front of the cab. Out of the corner of his eye he can see cabbie tightening up and then consciously relaxing. Zeb goes up to the entrance of the mid-rise, reverses in one fluid motion, yanks open the passenger door of the cab, leans in, and strikes a pressure point behind the cabbie's ear. The cabbie collapses against the wheel, out of service.

The watcher across the street stares in disbelief. This is not in the script. This was supposed to be a routine surveillance operation to watch out for the mark and report in when he turned up. He and his colleague are experienced agents and have taken down their share of badasses before, but the utter ease with which the mark has taken out his colleague shocks him. He hasn't seen anyone move so fast, changing from casual to lethal in a second. He calls his office and briefs them and is asked to check on his colleague but otherwise stay put, continue keeping a watch till others arrive.

He crosses the street to the cab and peers in. His colleague is unconscious but seems to be unharmed in any other way. He stands undecided for a moment, looking around the entrance to the building and around the street. He doesn't see the mark anywhere and thinks he has gone inside the building. He has lost sight of him.

Zeb has ducked down behind a few cars parked behind the cab, run back and crossed the street to the other side. He's now sitting in the same café in his former position. He has not made any efforts to hide himself and is in plain sight from the other side of the street. He knows what will happen now. What he doesn't know is what happens next once the cavalry show up.

They arrive half an hour later in a dark Lincoln and park behind the cab. By then, the cabbie has recovered and is chatting with the other watcher, no sign of any injury. A tall man steps out of the Lincoln's passenger seat, followed by the driver, and the four of them have a meeting. The tall man, the leader, looks at the building and up and down the street as the watchers speak. He issues instructions as he continues to scan the area and breaks off mid-speech when he spots Zeb across the street.

Zeb gives them a little wave and holds up his cappuccino.

There is a flurry of frantic discussion among the four of them, and then they head across the street. Zeb smiles at the way they spread themselves out as they near him.

'Have coffee, gentlemen, and rest your legs. I got tired just watching you.' Zeb relaxes, sprawling in his chair.

'FBI. Special Agent in Charge Isakson,' the tall man introduces himself with a clipped, controlled voice, but Zeb can detect the anger beneath the tone. 'I can have you arrested for assaulting a federal agent.'

'Me? Who did I assault? I went to the assistance of your agent, who seemed to be suffering from a nervous breakdown. I didn't touch him. As soon as I entered his cab, he fainted. I checked that he was okay and exited the cab. That's assault now, according to the FBI?'

Pressure-point unconsciousness sometimes plays havoc with short-term memory, and Zeb is banking that the driver doesn't remember much of what went on in the cab.

Isakson looks at his agent, who shrugs and looks embarrassed.

'Why are you guys watching for me?' Zeb asks.

'We wanted to talk to you in private, but since you've forced this,' Isakson says, 'we want you to back off your investigation. We want you to keep your distance from Holt. We want your sidekick, Broker, to not come sniffing around our systems for Holt's details. You have no idea what you're getting involved with, the various connecting threads, so back off.

'Remember, under the Patriot Act we have almost unlimited

powers. Suspects have been known to disappear indefinitely under this Act. And if you think your sister's connections will help you...she herself might come under the scrutiny of the Act,' continues Isakson, on not receiving any response from Zeb.

Zeb doesn't say a single word, nor move a muscle, yet Isakson feels the cold menace hitting him at the mention of his sister. He uneasily realizes why his colleagues told him not to go extreme on Zeb. He can sense his team shifting, spreading out, and dimly knows that Zeb could take them all out in a few seconds without breaking a sweat.

Isakson's hand automatically moves toward the lapel of his jacket, toward his shoulder holster. His hand stops when Zeb straightens and wordlessly points towards the Lincoln.

'Back off,' Isakson repeats and strides away, followed by his colleagues. He discreetly wipes his brow as he approaches the Lincoln.

Zeb watches them drive away. The warning is meaningless, and he has no intention of paying heed to it. Ever since leaving the Special Forces, he has done what he feels is right and has gone through people who opposed him.

People like Isakson.

Chapter 6

Rory is at Cassandra's apartment doing his homework when Zeb arrives. Rory bumps fists with him in passing and tells him, 'You're coming to dinner at our house. Aunt Cassie is, and so is Anne.'

'Can I say no?'

'Nope.' Rory grins.

Dinner is the usual cozy affair with Lauren and Anne bustling about serving great food. Anne is accompanied by her stockbroker boyfriend this time, a likeable guy exudes good humor.

Rory tells them about how Zeb's pitching practice has helped him get into his class's baseball team.

'All right, squirt,' says Connor when Rory has finished, 'it's time for the adults to talk now.'

Rory makes a face but goes to his room to play on his Xbox.

'I got back from the Congo a few days ago,' says Connor without preamble, 'and I think it's fair to say that over there feels like a different planet.

'I visited ten mines in the east and southeast, many of them gold and diamond mines. The treatment of women and children is shocking. Child labor is the norm; women are raped regularly by the mining authorities and militia – and this is just in the Western-owned mines. Alchemy, Hardinger's family company, owns three mines in the DRC, and I managed to visit all three of them and spoke extensively to the miners, the security guards, officers...all levels in the hierarchy.

'I expected the workers to be treated differently there; I am not naïve and have been around the world, to the sweatshops of Asia, South America, and the factories in China. But in the Congo, the workers are as good as slaves. I saw miners being whipped, children being beaten, and women being stripped of their clothes. These incidents happened every day at all the mines I visited.'

'How come you were able to wander freely in the mines and witness this?' Anne's boyfriend asks.

'I had a very expensive cover story prepared for me by the paper. I went in as a buyer of ore and had the word put out that I wasn't interested in how the mines were run. I had good backup, proof of funds, references, even my own security. So moving around the mines and seeing the operations openly wasn't an issue.'

He laughs. 'I had state-of-the-art stuff for recording – pen cameras that took stills and video in high resolution, button-hole recorders, all those gizmos – so I could record everything. In the evenings I used to mingle with the workers and talk to them as if I was looking to improve their conditions, and they spoke openly about their treatment. I used that same ploy with the employees of the mines, security, everybody.

'Hardinger's mines were run no differently from the other mines I visited. Child labor in all the mines, exploitation of women, and rampant brutality on display. In fact, some of the miners said that the mine near Kivu was hijacked by Alchemy's security company and thereafter claimed as Alchemy's own mine.'

He leans forward, his eyes glittering. 'I picked up rumors that there's an email trail between Hardinger and his mining officers about the mine hijacking and that he is aware of child labor. Imagine that. A high-profile senator, a fund-raiser for the President's party, who is complicit in the use of child labor, piracy of mines, and might have even sanctioned them. If I can get a paper trail linking him to those activities, it will be the end of the good Senator.'

Zeb is curious. 'Why is Hardinger attracting all your attention? Surely all mines in the Congo, in fact, all mines in Africa, must be indulging in these activities. Why aren't you going after all of them?'

'A lot of companies are Canadian-owned. I'll write about all Western-owned mines, but exposing Alchemy will have more impact, and that will, in turn, lead to more scrutiny of all the mines.

'And I know you're probably thinking that I'm going after Hardinger for the glory. There is that, I won't deny it. However, if the threats I've received from Hardinger's camp are any proof, then there is a smoking gun out there, and I aim to find it.

'My initial series of articles will be on the state of mining in Africa, and I will send the exposé with the focus on Alchemy and Hardinger. That should give me enough time to get the paper trail.'

'How serious are these threats?' asks Anne.

Connor shrugs. 'You get this in my profession, especially if you're going after someone high profile. There haven't been any direct threats. There never are. Just veiled references from people in his camp – saying my life will be easier if I focus on other issues...that these stories impact family too.

'There were a few anonymous calls asking me to drop my current story.'

Lauren is shocked. 'You never told me about those calls.'

'What's there to tell? They were anonymous calls. I used to get those when we were in Kentucky, remember?'

'But you never wrote about anyone so powerful.'

Connor snorts. 'This is my profession. I can't and won't turn tail at the first threat.'

'So, Major, what have you been up to since our last meeting?' Anne asks, changing the subject.

'Stopped three muggings, advised the Mayor on his security, and helped Matt Damon on some stunts for his movie,' replies Zeb.

A minute of stunned silence and then Connor laughs, then Anne, Lauren and the stockbroker follow. Cassandra smiles politely. She catches Zeb's eye. He shrugs.

'Well, well, Major. I didn't know humor was in your dictionary,' Anne comes back at him.

No reply from Zeb as he goes to the kitchen to fill up his glass. The stockbroker has noticed the byplay between Cassandra and Zeb.

'He wasn't joking, was he?'

Cassandra laughs out loudly and genuinely. 'Zeb hasn't joked in a century!'

'Advising the Mayor and Matt Damon, Zeb? I'm impressed!' the stockbroker exclaims on Zeb's return.

'Who are you? Batman?' Anne asks, finding it hard to believe.

'Just earning a living, ma'am.'

'The muggings? That's a living? You get paid per mugging prevention?'

'Things just happen when I'm about, ma'am.'

'That we can all believe!' Connor smiles widely, thinking, *I shouldn't be surprised. This is what he's good at and has a reputation for. I knew he worked with celebrities and public figures.* Connor comes back to his story. 'Zeb, do you think I should be doing anything about these threats? The last phone call was about a month ago.'

'You should find a way to record those calls, and if you

can't, then make a note of them and report them to the police. About the veiled threats, the same, ideally record them, or make a note of them. Take normal precautions, such as not being alone at night on the streets. Make sure Lauren or Rory are not alone at any time or with strangers. They will be your weak points.

'It's easy to become paranoid about these things. It comes down to how seriously you want to take these threats,' he continued.

'I have reported those calls to the police. Nothing much that they could do about them. They had no caller id, and a reverse call check revealed nothing. What would you do if you were in my position?' asks Connor.

'I would do what I told you,' answers Zeb. 'I would also look into arranging protection for Lauren and Rory till the threat disappeared.'

Lauren shivers. 'Why don't you drop this and write about something else?'

Connor shakes his head. 'I can't. This is what I do. This is my life.'

'When do your articles start appearing in the paper?' asks the stockbroker.

'A week from today and then every week, culminating in the article on Hardinger. Depending on what evidence I have by then, I'll submit it to the police and call for an investigation.'

'So in a few weeks, things will be jumping like a dog on hot chili.' The stockbroker smiles.

'You betcha, and Lauren will be going all frazzled. In Kentucky, when I broke the story on corruption and we became the center of attention, both welcome and unwelcome, Lauren ran for it. She took Rory with her and went to her folks. That's standing by your man for you.' Connor chortles.

'I did stand by you then...at a distance!'

'Oh yes, I nearly forgot,' Connor says. 'I got an invite for a fancy fund-raising dinner that Senator Hardinger is throwing for some charity. The dinner is free for any guests I bring along, and the newspaper is stumping up my attendance. How about going? All of us?'

'Moneybags' – Anne punches her boyfriend in the arm – 'and I are going to one of the Senator's dos, and I think that's the one. So we're already there. Maybe Cassandra and Zeb can join us? I presume you'll be taking Lauren along.'

'Cassandra's going with her friend with the juice, the Director,' Connor replies. 'Hey, maybe I can wangle an interview with her. What do you think, Cass?'

'Keep trying. Patience is a virtue.' Cassandra laughs.

'You know, we moved in next to you just because of your proximity to her so that I could get juicy scoops,' Conner declares. 'So far, that idea hasn't paid off.'

Lauren rolls her eyes. 'Zeb, will you join us?'

'I'm not into these things.'

'Oh, come on, Major, live it up. Surely the Mayor will already have invited you as a security consultant?' Anne mocks. 'And who knows, there might be ample opportunities there for you to play your heroic self.'

'I sense something here. Should I be jealous?' The stockbroker laughs.

'Relax, moneybags. Zeb isn't as rich as you. I just love pulling his leg,' replies Anne.

'Zeb, you are coming. You don't have a choice,' says Connor. 'Now about the camping.' He draws out a map. 'We go camping every year – the three of us, Anne, and moneybags, as she calls him, and this time Cass is going to join us,' he explains on seeing Zeb's raised eyebrows.

'This year we're going to the Catskills for a couple of weeks. Just us, nature and quiet.'

'And some bears,' shouts Rory from his room.

'They won't eat you, Rory. You're too sour for them,' Connor shouts back. 'He's been going on about the bears for ages. But the boy needs to toughen up. We're definitely going.'

'You joining us, Zeb?' Anne asks. 'You might be all that keeps us from being bear meat.'

'I'm feeling like bear meat now,' he replies.

Moneybags bursts into laughter. 'You were asking for that. But seriously, it would be great if you could join us, Zeb. The more the merrier.'

'Please, Zeb. These guys don't know how to keep me safe,' shouts Rory.

'That runt,' Connor mutters and quirks an eyebrow at Zeb. 'Well?'

'I'll let you know. I still have a few things to do.'

They break up once Connor has finalized the plans for their camping trip.

As Zeb and Cassandra make their way to her apartment,

she asks, 'You think you're being sucked into their plans?'

'As long as they leave me alone, I'm fine.'

'Are you getting pissed off at Anne?'

'She feels insecure around me. Picking on me is her defense mechanism. It's no big deal.'

Cassandra looks at him, jolted. *I didn't think he would figure her out so quickly and so deeply! Clare always said he was the most perceptive and aware person she had ever met. Now I know what she meant.*

The subway to Jackson Heights is almost empty when Zeb leaves Cassandra's apartment and boards it.

Holt is here, in the city, he thinks, as the subway carries him into darkness.

I can feel him.

Chapter 7

He meets Broker the next day. They haven't made any headway into tracing Holt's mother. The last few of the voice mails he left had called back, and none of them are her or anyone connected with Holt.

This time they meet at a café in Greenwich Village. Broker is wearing his countersurveillance glasses, sitting at a table on the sidewalk, his back to the wall. Many women and a few men give him a lingering glance as they walk past.

'I have word that someone wants to know who you are and has tried to get access to your file at the agency.' Broker continues, 'Now this could be anyone wanting to know who you are, or it could be Holt who got the word that I spread. I don't believe in coincidences, so let's assume it's Holt. Thing is, what if he comes after you?'

Zeb looks at him. 'That was sort of the point of letting Holt know that I'm hunting him.'

'What if he goes after Cassandra? He's not a person who adheres to any rules of engagement.'

'There is no record that Cassandra is related to me. The Director removed any connection in all my records. This was the condition under which I had undertaken some assignments.'

'Well, I know all about records. Don't forget, that's my specialty! And the Director, Andrews, and I know about her. That's too many people knowing, by my book,' Broker says dubiously.

'You know Bear and his lady, Chloe, don't you?' asks Zeb.

'Yep, I've sent some work his way. Come to think of it, I haven't heard much from him recently,' replies Broker.

'That's because he's looking after Cassandra. Him and his lady. They're good at body protection. So far they've just been looking out for her from afar, but I'm thinking of getting them to stay with her till this is over.'

Broker approves. 'You son of a gun. Always two steps ahead.'

'I called all the Holts in New Jersey, and none of them is Carsten Holt's mother. What if she changed her name or married again or retained her maiden name?' asks Zeb.

'Well then, we're up shit creek, aren't we? There would be no way of tracking her down. Don't forget that we're chasing a pretty slim lead based on the assumption that Holt is close to his mother and would want to stay nearby.'

'What if his mother has Holt as next of kin?' Zeb suggests. 'I know Cassandra has me down as her next of kin. Had. I got the records changed.'

Broker gives that thought and smiles slowly. 'That might just work. I'll write a program that searches land records, driving license databases, passports...all those that would need a next of kin. It might work, and at this point we haven't anything else to pursue.'

Broker has a very loose definition of what searching means. It often involves hacking – ethical hacking is how Broker describes it.

'You and I have been asked to back off from Holt. We could disappear, under the Patriot Act,' Zeb tells him and narrates his standoff with Isakson.

'That shit,' snorts Broker, 'does he think he can scare us? That we'll tuck our tails and stay quiet? That we'll forget?'

'Don't take Isakson and the Patriot Act lightly. I think you should stay away from this,' Zeb tells him.

Broker slams his palm on the table, the sound like a pistol shot echoing around the café, stilling it. He glares back at the other patrons looking their way.

'Bubba,' he looks back at Zeb and growls, 'this is the first and last time you say that.'

He looks away and composes himself. 'Now on Senator Hardinger and Alchemy. I think you know the history of the company, so I'll skip that stuff. Today the Senator and his family own 47% of the company through a complicated legal structure, but the Senator stepped down from the active running of the company once he was elected to the Senate. The company owns three mines in Africa and a few others in Australia, Latin America and Asia. Now the bad news. Holt and his associates are not on the payroll of Alchemy, not even as contractors.'

'They aren't listed here in the US as Alchemy's employees nor at any of Alchemy's companies in other countries. Just to be sure, I also checked the Senator's other business interests, and none of them list these guys.

'In Africa, the company employs several mercenaries or private military contractors, either directly or through security companies. These guys provide security for the mines and the officers. There is a rumor that the mine near Lake Kivu was actually hijacked by Alchemy's mercenaries, and then later legalized by Alchemy. The mine was previously run by the mom-and-pop-shop equivalent in the Congo, and the original owners were selling the ore to middlemen in the Congo. Alchemy, in one night, just replaced the entire operation with its own staff, paid the owners, and as far as the middlemen were concerned, nothing had changed. Not that they're too particular.'

'If the owners were paid off, why do you say the mine was hijacked?' asks Zeb.

'Don't forget, these are all rumors. Alchemy is not going to admit that they hijacked the mine, but there was a lot of media coverage in the DRC newspapers about a hijack. A lot of my contacts in that area confirmed it. The payment to the previous owners was to maintain a façade.

'They also bought off the media and the politicians there. What Alchemy did wasn't uncommon, and the hijack was soon forgotten.

'I have a list of all the military contractors employed by them directly as well as through their security companies. The list makes for interesting reading,' continues Broker.

He hands over a list with close to fifty names on it. He's organized the list based on name, demographics, and background. Zeb lingers over the background and notices that several of those are ex-Rangers or ex-Seals, and some of them could have served at the same time as the Rogue Six. He looks up at Broker, tapping the sheet.

'Yes, I know,' Broker says, 'but I'm not sure how that information helps us. It's too much to assume that all those Seals and Rangers know Holt, or were put there by Holt. All we can do now is just keep this at the back of our minds.'

'Have you told Cassandra about our hunt? And about Bear and Chloe?' Broker asks Zeb.

'Not yet. I will do so in the next few days.'

'Did Isakson tell you why he wanted you to back off Holt?'

'Nope. Andrews told me something about Holt giving them Al Qaeda intel in the Congo.'

Broker nods. 'Yes, that's what I've heard too, so you're at least getting the truth there, or what passes for the truth in those quarters.'

They part on that, Broker promising to call him once he's

made any progress on the hunt for Holt's mother.

The next day, Zeb digs up an ex-Seal who trained and served with Holt.

Buster 'Bunk' Talbot is now an arms dealer based in one of the toughest cities in New York. Newburgh. He's not particular who he sells to, and a lot of gangs from as far as Mexico and the West Coast give him their business. The gangs in Newburgh now protect him. He also is the first port of call for most mercenaries. He specializes in small arms and assault rifles.

Zeb drives a cab to Newburgh, after paying off the cab driver, and reaches the city in a couple of hours. A cab is less likely to be stolen or its wheels jacked than any other car. Newburgh sits pretty in the sun on the Hudson. He enters the city and drives along Broadway. With narrow streets running off Broadway, many of them dead ends, the city is made for crime. The run-down houses, ghettos, and abandoned parking lots – this is a city hope fled a long time back.

Zeb parks his cab on Broadway and walks down a narrow street. Bunk's outfit is at the far end of that street, at a dead end with a good firing line over the alley if he has to withstand a siege. Zeb can feel people looking at him from behind the boarded doors of the abandoned houses – most likely the gang members protecting Talbot.

Talbot's gun shop would make an armory proud. Gleaming glass cases house pistols of all kinds, ammunition neatly laid out, combat rifles arranged in racks, new metal and gun oil hanging heavy in the air, and even a small firing range at the back of the shop.

Talbot knows why Zeb is here. Zeb had let him know he was coming, and in the circles he moves in, there are few secrets. Talbot has built a nice business here; the gangs and mercenaries pay cash and keep trouble in check. He sells to rival gangs, and they have no qualms about it. They know he sells the best weapons and is always able to get them in the quantities they want. He has spoken to some Special Forces friends of his about Zeb, and they've all said Zeb isn't someone anyone wants on their case.

He makes Zeb wait a long time before seeing him. Zeb is used to such power games, and it makes no difference to him.

'Dude, I know what you want, and I have no idea where he is. I sell guns. I don't sell information, even if I had it. Now if you're looking for a gun, we can talk.'

'Did you outfit Holt?' Zeb asks, looking around the gun shop.

'No comment. Dude, if you want to buy something, let's talk, or else get out. Don't waste my time. You're bad for business. This town's infested with gangs – my customers, by the way – who'll think you're the FBI or the cops. The only reason I've wasted the last few minutes of my life talking to you is because we both served.'

'You have a good setup here. How have you managed to stay under the cops' radar? I bet they'd be interested in your clientele,' says Zeb, ignoring what Talbot has been saying.

Talbot slaps a hand on the counter, the guns on the wall rattling with the report and drawing looks from the group at the firing range. He glares at them, and they get back to business. Turning to Zeb, he says, 'Carter, look into my eyes. Read my lips. I am not interested in talking to you unless you're buying. And even then, I'm not sure I want your business.'

Zeb looks at him for a long time. 'Tell Holt I am coming. Tell him I was the one in the hut. He'll know what I'm referring to.'

Talbot laughs. 'There's such a thing as a phone, you know. You could've told me all this on the phone. Not that it makes any difference to me and not that I'm going to do what you say, anyway. Holt and I served together a long time back. I have no contact with him now. And even if I did, I wouldn't be your go-between over whatever bug you have up your ass about him. Now why don't you vamoose before I take a more active role in ejecting you from my shop?'

'Tell him,' says Zeb. He leaves, knowing that Holt will be getting his message from Talbot shortly. The Seals bond is unbreakable, and it has an active network.

Out in the street, word of his altercation with Talbot seems to have spread. Several gang members are hanging around the street, giving him the stink eye.

Zeb is amused by their posturing and wonders how many of them will live to see another year. He glides like oiled steel through the heat of their gazes, not one daring to stop him.

On reaching New York, Zeb has the urge to visit his old tabla school in Jamaica. He can hear dimly the sounds of the tabla through the outer doors, and once he enters, he is awash in the sounds and smell of the drums. A bunch of young kids are seated around a frail old Indian man, with a full head of hair, keen eyes and strong fingers. His teacher, who on spotting Zeb, flashes a warm smile. Zeb sits against a far wall, with folded knees, and listens.

'The tabla is empty, hollow, for a reason.' His teacher beckons Zeb to sit next to him, takes the dagga, and places it in front of him and the kids.

'Playing the tabla is easy. Once you learn the techniques, you can play it. But if you feel the tabla, if you allow it to speak, then it will allow you to fill it up. That's why it is hollow, so that you can create and fill it up.' He strikes the syahi of the dagga and produces a deep tone. He motions Zeb to sit beside him and offers him a pair of tablas. He draws another pair for himself and leads off on a taal.

Zeb follows, and teacher and student fill themselves with rhythm.

Chapter 8

He meets Bear and his partner the next day and outlines the circumstances to them. They agree about the need for close protection; they've been doing this for several years and can read a situation well.

Cassandra is furious when she learns about Zeb's plans for Bear and his partner to protect her, shadow her, for an indefinite length of time. Zeb is vague about the reasons for their presence.

'What is the worst that will happen to me?' she shouts. 'Someone will come and do me harm? So what? I am not prepared to be followed by a gorilla and his mate and have them cramp my life.'

Zeb ignores her.

'Zeb, don't stonewall me. I will not have them around. After living in a bloodthirsty city like D.C., do you think your enemies scare me?'

Zeb doesn't doubt that bit. Cassandra has faced down muggers, survived bar fights, and talked down a gun-wielding hostage-taker, all courtesy of living in D.C. But all that cannot be compared to the ruthlessness that Holt brings to the table. Zeb isn't taking any chances. He continues to ignore her, and she finally stomps out and slams her bedroom door behind her.

Bear coughs politely. 'Gee, that went well. Do you think she's gonna be difficult?'

'Nope, she'll be fine by tomorrow. By the way, she doesn't know that you've already been shadowing her for weeks...so it might be best if you kept that to yourselves.'

He shows them around the apartment and his arms cache. He'd built a hidden compartment by knocking out a section of the wall, covering the inside of it with soft velvet and rebuilding a hinged door on it that looks exactly like the wall. It can be opened only by specific pressure on three pressure points in a particular sequence. Cassandra doesn't know it's there. Zeb has several of these scattered around the city, complete with new identities and bundles of cash.

Bear whistles when he sees the Glock 19, Smith and Wesson .357 SIG, a Steyr S40-A1, a Heckler and Koch HK416, CS Gas, stacks of ammunition, hunting knives and even some flashbangs and sting grenades.

'Enough to start a war,' he grunts.

'Or survive one,' Chloe replies.

'We have our own kit, but it's good to know that this is around,' Bear continues. 'We've cased the building and the neighborhood in the last few weeks, and we're good to go from tonight.'

Zeb briefs them on the neighbors, the doorman, and various routines in the building, and works out call codes with them.

As he prepares to leave, Rory rushes in. He comes to an abrupt halt and gapes at Bear. Bear is huge, towers over Zeb by a foot, is built like a fortress, and sports a full beard; Chloe is just the opposite, petite and svelte.

Bear returns his stare and then winks slowly at Rory. He holds out a hand and introduces himself, 'You must be Rory. For some strange reason I've never been able to understand, all my friends call me Bear.' A twitch of a smile. 'This is my partner, Chloe. We'll be staying at your Aunt Cassandra's place for a few weeks.'

Rory giggles in spite of himself and looks at Zeb.

'Cass needs some help, and Bear and Chloe pitched in. They're good friends of mine. Bear is a better pitcher than I am, by the way, and knows more about baseball than anyone else I know.'

That swings it for Rory, and he rushes out to tell his mother. Zeb looks at Bear and Chloe. 'Let me introduce you to the rest of them.'

He brings them next door and introduces them to Lauren. Lauren's eyes are full of questions, but Zeb says he'll explain later when Connor is home. He leaves Bear and Chloe to sort things out with Lauren, and then later, with Cassandra.

He walks back to the subway; flowing through the anonymous passengers calms him and helps him think. He knows what he's doing: using himself as bait to draw in and apply pressure to Holt. He knows Holt is in the city. He doesn't know how he knows, but the knowledge is there. He has always had that tingling awareness when his prey is nearby. He tried explaining this to psychologists when he was in the Special Forces, but they didn't get it. Since then, he hasn't told anyone else about it, though he thinks Broker and Bear might have sensed it in him. They are two with whom he has come closest to lowering his guard.

He checks his phone and sees a message from Broker. 'Jackpot,' he shouts when Zeb calls him. 'I got the mother of the fucker! Her name is Pamela Whitlock; her address is in Williamstown – about an hour and a half away from Jackson. She married again and changed her name to Whitlock. No kids and she willed the family home in Jackson to Holt. That's how I got her.' All coming in a rush from Broker as he enjoys his high.

'Her second husband passed away a few years back. No known income right now, except a state pension. I guess her husband left her a decent pile to live off.

'You want to check her house out? I know you want to, and this time I'm coming along with you,' Broker says.

'Don't get involved. This has nothing to do with you.'

'Bubba, we've had this discussion before. I got involved the day I met you. It's not as if I haven't been in the field ever since I started dealing in information.'

Zeb is aware of this.

Broker has been on a few missions with other military contractors, though he picks and chooses his missions. If he has to choose a partner, Broker will be his first choice, rock steady under fire, cool head, and a first-rate sniper. For an analyst, Broker has a knack for using a long gun.

He could do with a second pair of eyes, but doesn't want to involve anyone else in this. As it is, there are too many non-principals involved.

'Bubba, I know what you're thinking, but there's no way you're going to Williamstown alone. I *am* coming along with you.'

Silence on the line, then Broker continues, 'I'll outfit a vehicle tomorrow, and we can go. Right now all we want to do is check the place out and see if we can pick up any sign of Holt there.'

Zeb looks out the window. If Holt is staying with his mother, then that could be a complication. Zeb has never strayed from his rule of not involving non-principals.

He also wonders if Mendes and Jones are with Holt. He thinks it's a strong possibility. The six of them were working together a long time, and the events in the DRC would only bind them closer together. Holt still remains his priority, since he was the ringleader, and once he finds Holt, he can turn his attention to the others.

Broker drives up in an anonymous Honda Civic with New Jersey plates the next day. Zeb inspects the car and sees that he has kitted it out with a parabolic mike, infrared binoculars, a fiber-optic camera and recorder, and a thermal imager.

'I love technology,' he says defensively when Zeb looks across at him. 'Besides, these will be useful.'

'Is this your car?' Zeb asks.

'One of them. You know I have a car rental agency, which is a front for my cars. It's easier and offers anonymity as well as control.'

Zeb thinks for a moment. 'Let's go back to the rental agency and change the rental name to mine. I also want your agent to have a good look at me.'

Broker looks at Zeb as if he just sang 'I'm a Little Teapot' while wearing a pink tutu and Spock ears.

Zeb looks back at him.

Broker snaps his fingers. 'Gotcha. If Holt trails back, you want him to know it's you.'

Zeb nods. 'That's why I don't want you involved. This has nothing to do with you.'

Broker snorts. 'Let's get going. Enough wasting time on this. And don't bring this up again.'

They drive to the rental agency, where Zeb walks in and changes the rental name and hangs around aimlessly, checking out the flyers on the walls, making sure he is visible to the CCTV cameras mounted inside the agency.

They drive off once they're done, with Broker at the wheel. 'So how do you want to play this?' he asks. 'We can just do a few passes by the house, we can stay till dark and break in, or we can mount long-term surveillance with a few others... there are many ways.

'And what will you do once you find Holt?' he pushes on before Zeb can reply. 'For all your badass rep, you were never the cold-blooded execution type.'

'Are you done?'

'Just.'

'We are not going to do anything you've suggested. We're parking right opposite her house to sit for a few hours.'

'I figured you were going to say something like that. Do you know what a spoilsport you are, Zeb? All these gadgets... when am I going to get to use them?

'And what will you do once you find him? What if you

come across him in the subway? You can't take him to the Feds because they told you to back off. They might, in fact, go after you. If the cops get him, they'll just hand him over to them. Other than the execution option, I don't see a Plan B *or* a Plan C.'

'I'll be handing him over to the DRC's Embassy.'

Broker sits in stunned silence for a beat, then laughs long and loud – right into New Jersey.

Chapter 9

They reach Williamstown close to noon. A small town with barely twenty thousand people, a town that can be driven through in an hour and forgotten in less than that. A town for retirees and those who want to escape the rapidity of large cities. They find Pamela Whitlock's home without much difficulty and make a few passes in front of it. The house is set back from the street and is surrounded by foliage. Broker has the house blueprints, so they look them over – it's a six bedroom with front and back gardens. The gardens are surrounded by tall trees and have an exit to the side. Broker has activated the body-heat detector in his Civic, and it comes up empty. No one in the house...or nothing the machine can detect.

A B&E in a residential area such as this is always high risk. Neighbors know each other, strangers stand out, and residents gossip – not to mention the Block or Neighborhood Watches. Whitlock's house has the saving graces of being set back a distance and surrounded by dense foliage. The streetlights are covered with grime, their illumination poor. Though Zeb has no intention of breaking in, force of habit makes him automatically seek out entry and exit points.

They park on the street, just to the left, still visible to anyone inside the house. Zeb makes himself conspicuous by getting out of the car, staring long and hard at the house, then walking past the place a few times, making a show of taking notes and photos as he observes the structure.

'The house looks empty, feels empty, and the machine says it's empty. You're just hoping that the neighbors spot you and get the word to his mother and from her lips to Holt's ear. All this dicking around...Zeb, I thought you were a man of action,' grumbles Broker as he settles in the car and prepares to snooze.

Zeb spends a couple of hours on the street. In that time a neighbor comes back from shopping, the kids piling into the house with the parents following, staring curiously at Zeb. A patrol car passes him, slowly, once and then twice, but does not stop. A few other cars pass by, all with New Jersey plates.

They leave in the late afternoon, Broker driving, all the while grumbling about the waste of time.

'Happy? Now that you've made yourself a target, painted

yourself bright orange?' asks Broker as they reenter New York.

'There isn't any other way,' says Zeb, 'if I want him to come to me.'

Broker throws up his hands in frustration. 'I'll keep plugging away at my databases, on my network, and also keep at it on Hardinger. If anything turns up, I'll let you know. Do you want me to check into Mendes and Jones?'

Zeb shakes his head.

Broker leaves Zeb at Jackson Heights, a few blocks away from his apartment. Zeb uses the walk to run through what he has so far and to plan his next move.

He has two choices at this stage – keep hunting for Holt's whereabouts, which might be a long, drawn-out process during which Holt could escape from the country, or draw Holt out by being provocative. Zeb being Zeb, has taken the provocative option by hanging around his mother's house, without being directly aggressive, below the cops' and the FBI's radar. There is no guarantee that his actions will work nor that Broker's digging might find Holt, but Zeb has to run with what he has, and his hunting instincts tell him that Holt will come after him.

It's what he would have done, had he been in Holt's position.

He goes to his apartment and takes out his carryall, which has all his weapons – a Glock 17, a Beretta 92A1, a HK416 as well as a Heckler and Koch G28, a Benchmade spring-loaded Entourage knife, some flashbangs, his cable camera – and makes a lightweight pack of his clothes. He will be living in rundown seedy hotels, where there's no one to note his comings and goings, till this blows over. He takes out a map and works out a grid of blocks between 58th and 25th Street. Broker had hired the Civic within that grid, and it will give Holt a starting point for locating Zeb.

He walks into a hotel near 58th Street on the West Side and checks in. The porter does not look up from the football game playing on his TV as he wordlessly takes Zeb's money and hands over a key. The room is surprisingly clean and well organized, with a small, well-maintained bathroom and a tiny window overlooking the street. He freshens up and explores the hotel thoroughly, noting the fire escape next to his window, the rear exit, the lighting along the corridors, and the single camera facing the entrance.

He walks around the block and familiarizes himself with its layout.

He then walks to that perennially populous place in New York City, Times Square, and hangs out, watching the ebb and flow of people, the pulse of the city throbbing.

The next day he hires the same Civic from the same agency, drives out to Williamstown, and repeats his observation of Holt's mother's home.

He notices the neighbor's curtain twitching when he has spent an hour there, but the thermal imager is quiet.

He leaves after another hour. On returning to the city, he checks out of the hotel and finds another anonymous one a few streets south.

He walks the streets of the city the next few days, and it is on the fourth day that violence finds him.

* * *

He's walking along East 36th Street late at night, not many pedestrians around, barring the lone cab cruising the street and the occasional insomniac dog walker. He hears a scuffle ahead and slows down further, checking out the street ahead and behind him. Nothing. Empty.

He moves cautiously to the mouth of the alley from which the sounds come.

Sniffen Court is one of the few alleys in lower Manhattan. It was built in the mid-nineteenth century for stables, which were later converted to housing. The far end of the alley is a dead end, with a brick wall punctuating it like a period. Adorning the brick wall are plaques of Greek horsemen. The alley is lined with genteel townhouses, where time moves just a little slower than the rest of the city.

Normally the alley is fenced off by a metal gate, but tonight the gate is wide open, and Zeb can see three black men holding a black man and white woman at gun and knife point.

All five of them are in the shadow of a house lower down the alley, and the houses either seem to be empty, or the inhabitants are unable to hear the scuffling. Zeb is wearing dark clothes and is a shadow amongst the many shadows on East 36th. He watches the scuffling a long time and also the alley behind them for signs of a trap. He doesn't detect any. One of the attackers is holding the black man at knife point, the knife pricking his neck; the other two are grappling with the woman, covering her face so she can't make any sound. A mugging seems to have turned into attempted rape.

Zeb steps inside the alley with his back to a wall and moves within visible sighting distance of the five. The woman sees him, and her eyes go wide, and her struggling draws the attention of the attackers.

'Beat it, nigga,' one of them mutters. 'This is a private party.'

Zeb steps forward. Three to one, not the best odds, but usually if the ringleader is taken out, the others run. Been proven since the days of kings.

One of the black men swings away from the woman and advances towards Zeb, his gun glinting in the shadowed light. 'Last chance, asshole, mind your own business and you get to live.'

Not the leader, a minion; still, taking the minion out would whittle them down to two.

He takes a step back, closer to the wall, to put distance between him and the rest, and the attacker follows, his finger on the trigger, slack. Zeb can see the black bore swing toward him and takes another step back toward the wall. If the gun fires, it will either hit him or the wall. Acceptable.

The black man steps forward, grinning at seeing Zeb cornered against the wall.

The hand of a good martial arts practitioner can move at about forty-six feet per second. Martial artists have to be slowed down or the movie camera speeded up to capture their action sequence for a movie and played back at twenty-four frames a second, or else all that the audience will see is a blur.

At forty-six feet per second, the martial artist delivers nearly forty-six joules of energy in an overhand strike. The energy needed to break the ribs of an average person is thirty joules. Much less is needed to break a wrist.

The black man doesn't see Zeb's left hand move. All he feels is a massive block of concrete striking his wrist, and the gun falls and skitters away. His brain takes a few seconds to process that his wrist has been broken, and then intense pain strikes him. A strike to the ribs and he collapses.

The black man holding the woman looks at them for a moment; she sees her chance and screams loudly for help. Despite her terror, her eyes are riveted on Zeb. She thinks he'll be shot, but the next moment the black man has fallen to the ground, Zeb standing tall over him, his eyes dark, empty, staring into hers.

He glides to the one holding her boyfriend; a strike to the neck and a wrist lock and he is on the ground.

The black man who was holding her stumbles to his feet and flees, and she sees that her rescuer makes no attempt to stop him. In fact, he takes a step back and lets the remaining two black men get up and stumble away too.

He asks them, 'I can catch them. Do you want to call the cops?'

'We were just strolling; these guys were hiding in this alley and sprang on us. They took our money, our cards and were looking to take my jewelry when you came in.' Fear and adrenaline push the words out from her.

By now the alley has come alive; several doors have opened, the residents emerging from their cocoons. One of them has called the cops, and they can hear the sirens in the distance. The residents surround the couple, and a bubble of excited chatter envelops them. The woman looks up after a few moments to point out Zeb to the residents and thank him, but he's gone. She goes to the mouth of the alley and looks around the street, but all she can see is shadows and deep darkness.

The cops do a perfunctory round of questioning, but in the absence of the attackers and the rescuer, there isn't much more they can do.

Silence descends as the residents disappear into their homes and the cops take the couple away. Zeb emerges from a recessed doorway down East 36th and walks away into the dark. Broker calls it his Batman syndrome, with a difference: Batman hunted trouble. Trouble hunts Zeb.

Chapter 10

Zeb has nearly forgotten that he has agreed to join Connor's party to attend Hardinger's fundraiser. Rory's excited message on his phone reminds him. He checks out of his hotel, finds another one equally anonymous in the square of blocks, checks in, and then proceeds to Cassandra's apartment.

Zeb has had to rent a tux for the occasion. At Connor's place, he finds everyone gathered awaiting him, except for Cassandra. She has gone ahead with the Director. She has let Bear and Chloe go, since the Director has her own security detail around her.

Anne lets out a whistle when she sees Zeb. 'My, my, Major. Don't *you* clean up nice!'

Rory giggles.

'Enough of that, children,' Connor says as he pushes them toward the door.

They take two cabs, with Zeb sharing with Anne and her boyfriend to the $1000-a-plate charity fundraiser in downtown Manhattan.

Security is tight and professional, as it has to be with several celebrities and national politicians present. Zeb separates from his main group and hugs a wall, observing the events and the people.

Hardinger is easy to spot since he's hosting the event and is never far from center stage. Tall, handsome, tanned, white teeth smiling and a full head of hair: he has all the physical attributes of a successful politician. Zeb has gone through his backstory and knows that he was a marine once and has seen combat.

Hardinger has security posted discreetly around the hall. He's probably hired special event security for the evening. Some of the security detail carry the veteran look, but none of them are from the dossier Broker gave him.

He scans the guests, doesn't recognize most of them, which doesn't surprise him. He has only a casual interest in politics and the Hollywood scene.

He sees Cassandra and the Director seated together; she seems to feel his look, turns around, spots him, and sends a brief smile his way. She gestures that she wants to talk to him afterward. Connor, Lauren, Anne, and her boyfriend are seated together. They've left Rory with a babysitter.

Hardinger is a consummate host, engaging with the audience easily, using a brand of self-deprecating humor to pepper the evening's festivities.

Connor signals for him to join them at the dinner table once the serious business is done. 'How are you finding it, Major?'

'It's my first event of this kind, so I have no benchmark.'

'Zeb never has any benchmark in any case. He doesn't compare. He treats everything as a solitary incident,' interjects a voice behind them.

Broker.

Zeb makes the introductions and asks him, 'I thought Internet forums were your hangout?'

'And I thought the martial arts schools were yours.'

'So how do the two of you know each other?' asks Anne.

'We bumped into each other in Somalia. I was an intelligence analyst, and Zeb, well, Zeb was just drifting,' replies Broker with a broad smile.

'I have to say I find this event very polished and sophisticated. But then I would expect nothing less given Hardinger's standing. It's easy to see how he has become one of the foremost politicians in the country,' Connor says, bringing the topic back to the evening.

'You seem to admire him, bro...better be careful. You might end up dropping your story on his company.' Anne laughs.

'No fear of that. I admire his smoothness, but the story is still alive and heating up. I have some interesting emails from him to his staff in Africa about working conditions and acquiring new mines. Nothing that implicates him directly yet, but one could read a lot between the lines if one chose to do so. The emails are now with my legal department to determine if we can go with the story. But I'm also hoping to get further info from my sources, so fingers crossed.'

'Talking about me?' a rich baritone booms behind them, and Hardinger appears, clapping a hand on Connor's shoulder.

'How are you, Connor? Having a good time? Who are your friends?' he asks, flashing a super-white grin at all of them.

'Good show here, Senator. No wonder the party has so much faith in you when it comes to fundraising,' replies Connor, introducing the rest of his party.

'Major, huh? Landlubber! I guess someone has to do that job. I mean, carrying our bags while we did the fighting.' The

Senator smiles at Zeb to take the sting out of his words.

Hardinger guides them, without appearing to do so, to the gallery at the far end. One end of the gallery has photographs of the Senator with the President, the Speaker of the House, various international leaders, news clippings...the tough life of a politician. At the opposite end are photographs of him during his marine days and his medals.

Anne murmurs, 'Nice touch. One end he's doing good for the country; the other end he's fighting for it.'

Zeb has to agree. Hardinger with his sniper rifle, posing in various countries of the world, is made for marine recruitment posters.

'So, Connor, how did your Africa trip go?' asks the Senator.

'It was good, got good background for the series I'm working on.'

'The exposé of the mining industry there? Their working practices and their use of labor?'

'You know very well what I'm working on. Doesn't Alchemy have some mines in the Congo?'

'Yes, and if you're implying that Alchemy is perpetrating any wrongdoing, I'll tell you now that I have no idea what their practices are. I'm no longer running it, but I ran a clean ship when I was there.'

'Time will tell.'

The Senator stands in front of his marine sniper photographs. 'You know, Connor, one of the reasons I loved being a sniper was that collateral damage is minimal. But there is always collateral damage in any profession, and a responsible person should take steps to minimize it.

'Don't you agree, Major?' he adds, turning to Zeb.

'I was just the bag handler back in the day, Senator. What do I know of these big terms?' Zeb replies. He's eyeing the Purple Heart, the Silver Star, and various sniper-award citations on display.

'You any good with a long gun, Major?' asks Hardinger.

'Yup, at using them as a crutch.'

Hardinger gives a short bark of laughter. 'I sense hidden depths in you, Major. I can easily find your service record if I want to.'

'If you find anything of interest, let me know. Maybe we can swap secrets.'

Hardinger smiles. 'Have a good time, folks. I have to get

back to urging people to open their wallets.' He walks away.

Connor watches him. 'I would love to bring him down.'

'What if you aren't able to dig up any dirt on Hardinger? Will you can the story?' Lauren asks.

'Nope. The story goes ahead whatever happens. After all, it *is* about the mining practices of Western-owned mines.'

'That's good,' says Lauren with relief. 'I thought you were losing your objectivity on this story.'

'Won't happen. I'm after my Pulitzer.' He chuckles. 'Come on. Let's see what's in store for the rest of the evening.'

He shepherds all of them back to their seats. Anne glances back and sees Broker lost in thought in front of the Senator's medals.

* * *

It was hot in Mogadishu, almost ninety degrees, the dry weather sucking all moisture from the body. Broker was attached to a Rangers patrol and had been in the city for a few months. They were there to capture General Aidid, who was becoming a major nuisance to peace and the UN-recognized government of Somalia. This was a war sanctioned by the UN, but had been severely hampered by the poor quality of intelligence generated by the US forces.

Broker had been deployed to the Rangers unit to change that. He had been there a couple of months, and they had already lost a couple of Rangers to Somalian snipers.

That day they were driving in an armored Jeep along the dusty lanes of Mogadishu. Broker had been the last to board the Jeep and was seated closest to the rear, five others in front of him. He had been ribbed a lot for that, the usual ribbing that intel guys got from field soldiers.

They rocketed down a dusty road, buildings alongside them. Broker had noticed a green and white hotel, a two-story basic building that they were just passing. The far end of the hotel opened into a crossroad. There weren't any pedestrians in the heat. The burnt-out shell of a car in front of the hotel was the sole occupant.

In Mogadishu, dusty, slumbering streets were the battlefields.

A Somali attired in plain clothes, his face covered by a red towel, stepped from behind the car wreck, holding an RPG launcher in his hand. Broker gaped in disbelief. One second the street was empty, peaceful, the next second there's this

Somali standing there with dust motes swirling around him and death in his hands.

The Jeep braked suddenly, the Ranger Sergeant shouting, 'Cover. Cover. Rocket.'

Broker scrambled off the back, stumbling, recovering himself, and ran toward the wall of the hotel, a recessed doorway, whatever cover he could find, even as he heard the distinctive thump of the launcher. A moment later the Jeep lifted off and was flung against the hotel walls. A blast of heat hit him, followed by the Jeep pinning him, its sidewall and roof lying across his waist and legs.

Broker blacked out for a minute, and when he came to, he saw that the Ranger driver of the Jeep had taken the blast full-on, his remains lying on the road. As soon as launcher guy had fired, he was joined by several Somalis who had laid down more fire on the Americans behind the burning Jeep.

His eyesight blurred and hazy with sweat, Broker scrambled for his rifle, which was lying a few feet away, but his body wouldn't move an inch. He didn't know how badly he was crushed; his body was pumping adrenaline in massive doses, keeping the pain at bay.

He turned his head slowly toward the Rangers and saw three of them still alive, the Sergeant barking furiously in his radio and the two others returning fire. All of them damaged but alive. Farther away lay the body of the fourth Ranger, who wouldn't be returning fire, or anything else, anymore.

Broker stretched for his rifle, his fingers scraping in the dirt, blood roaring in his ears. Dimly he heard the Sergeant screaming, 'Cover. Cover,' and turned to see launcher guy raising the barrel of the launcher toward them as the other Somalis raised a heavy cover fire.

Launcher guy's head disappeared in a pink mist. Broker thought one of the Rangers got him, and then he heard another flat crack, and another Somali head disappeared. Broker turned his head, thinking the cavalry had arrived, but couldn't see anyone. The dusty street was empty save for heat waves.

Evenly spaced shots, no hurry, a professional, thought Broker dimly, as the flat cracks continued and the Somalis fell. The shooting stopped as the last Somali dropped. Silence filled the street, nothing moved, and then a tall silhouette emerged through the dust waves and stood over Broker.

Silently, he bent down and pushed at the carcass of the Jeep. The remaining Rangers rushed to help him, and they freed Broker.

'Thanks, dude. We'd be at the Pearly Gates by now if you hadn't showed up.' The Sergeant looked at the stranger. 'Which unit are you with?'

The stranger kept silent and walked away, his sniper rifle an extension of him.

Zeb.

Broker had gone back to the site later when he had recovered – he would have the slightest limp for the rest of his life – and retraced their movements and Zeb's. Zeb had been walking on the roof of a building when he heard the ambush. Broker could see his footsteps paced evenly on the dust film covering the roof, and then the footsteps lengthened as Zeb began to run. He saw where Zeb had kneeled on the roof and taken his first shot, the one that took out launcher guy. Broker estimated the distance to be close to 1000 yards. Under pressure, kneeling, 1000 yards and the first shot had scored. Broker knew only a handful of men in the world who could make that shot. Broker remembered that each of the subsequent shots had been unhurried, Zeb taking his time despite the obvious pressure on him.

* * *

A tap on his shoulder rouses Broker from his reverie.

'You were far away. Joining us?' Anne asks.

Broker makes his way to their group, but Zeb is missing. He's hugging the wall again and scanning the room ceaselessly. The event holds no interest for him.

Broker joins him after a while. 'Recognize any of them?'

Zeb shakes his head.

'Me neither,' replies Broker, 'but then I wasn't really expecting any of them to be here. Holt might be a twisted son of a bitch, but he's not a stupid twisted son of a bitch, and that's assuming there is a link between Holt and Hardinger.'

'He sent a message for you.' Broker grins when he feels Zeb still like a cat. 'Remember that washed-up veteran you spoke to?'

'Kelly.'

'Yup, Kelly. I think you asked him to spread the word that you're hunting Holt?'

Zeb nods.

'Well, he got passed a message from his network.' Broker pauses for effect and then gives up, seeing that Zeb can outwait the Sphinx.

'He told Kelly that you can forget about hunting him. He's coming after you.'

He waits for a reaction. Gets none.

'Well, isn't that what you wanted? Exactly that reaction?'

'Yes, but until he shows up, this is meaningless. In fact, I'm surprised he even bothered to send this message. How do you know it's from him?'

Broker turns serious. 'Kelly was told to pass on that the girl with the burning hair who you found alive? He left her dead.'

Zeb says nothing, shows nothing. Not even Andrews knew about the girl with the burned hair, only someone on the scene would, and also know that Zeb moved her away from the fire. Someone. Holt or his remaining colleagues.

Broker sees no reaction from Zeb, but from his very stillness he knows there is a blast furnace raging inside him.

'That helps,' says Zeb finally, 'but it doesn't change anything. The plan is still to draw him out to me.'

'I would say you're niggling away at him seems to be working if he's resorting to messages like that,' agrees Broker. 'Do you want to pass any message back to Holt?'

'Nope.'

They watch the party in silence, and then Broker nudges Zeb. 'The Director.'

Zeb looks across and sees her raising an eyebrow at him. He makes his way across.

'You don't take orders, do you?'

'Ma'am, I am shocked. I have never disobeyed an order in my life,' he replies, straight-faced.

'Be careful. You're alone in this. You're going up against an establishment that I can't save you from.'

'Not a new situation to me,' Zeb replies and makes his way back.

Broker snorts in derision when Zeb updates him. 'Funny how in the grand scheme of things, what happened in the Congo gets forgotten, or gets buried. Bureaucrats. Used toilet paper rolls have more value.'

Broker turns serious. 'You might find it's not just Holt gunning for you. The establishment' – he waves a hand around him – 'might want to bury all loose ends along with the story.'

Zeb nods once; he's aware of that. They join Connor once the events have finished and make their way out.

'Major, you're coming to the Catskills with us next week, aren't you?' Anne asks.

'I have a lot on my plate,' replies Zeb.

'Rory will be so disappointed. He was looking forward to having you there. Can't you try, Zeb?' Lauren asks him.

'I'll give it some thought and let you know in a couple of days.'

He goes back with Broker, who turns to him while driving, 'You worried that Holt might attack when you guys are in the mountains?'

'Yes. And also I don't want Rory to get too close to me. You know very well I'm not cut out for these things. The closer I am to people, the greater the risk I put them in.'

Silence fills the car.

'A long time ago, I knew someone who used to never turn his back on relationships, whatever the circumstances.'

More silence.

As they're nearing Jackson Heights, Broker asks him, 'What will you be doing now? Provoking Holt some more?'

'I'm meeting the FBI.'

Chapter 11

'W hat? Why?' Broker exclaims. 'The Director and I spoke at length tonight.'

'I'm confused, man. You were at her table not more than five minutes. I was watching.'

'We spoke outside the hall, when she was coming out of the restroom. But the how and where is irrelevant.'

'Right, so what was she saying about them? And why couldn't they contact you directly?'

'Mendes wants to talk to the FBI. That's thrown them in a loop, since they're already talking to Holt.'

'So?'

'So, they want to talk to me first.'

'About?'

'No idea. The Director asked me to meet them as a favor to her.'

Broker mulls this over. 'You know it might be a setup.'

'Yep.'

'You know you're not the FBI's poster boy. They could make you disappear under the Patriot Act.'

'Everything is a setup to you.'

'In my information business, it doesn't pay to take things at face value. You're really going to meet them?'

'Yep.'

'Maybe I should come along as backup.'

'Maybe you shouldn't.'

Zeb meets Isakson at Federal Plaza after being made to wait for far too long and then patted down and searched thoroughly. Isakson's payback for humiliating him.

Isakson places a folder in front of him. 'I think you've met Pieter Mendes. Ex-Ranger was in the Congo, and now in New York.'

Zeb opens the folder and idly flips through it. It has the same information in it that Andrews, and later on Broker, had provided him with. 'Never met him. Name doesn't ring a bell either.'

Isakson pauses. 'Come, come now, Major. Let's stop playing games, shall we? We know what you did in the Congo. Our brothers in the agency whispered in our ears.

'After we leaned on them,' he adds.

'Don't waste my time with stuff you and I already know,'

Zeb replies and gets up to leave.

Isakson steps forward. 'You're not going anywhere.' He steps back when he sees Zeb's expression.

'We need your help,' he says finally, after a long silence. 'We've been receiving a steady stream of intel from Holt on Al Qaeda's activities in the Congo. This intel has helped us close in on some dangerous networks. As you are aware, in return we have offered Holt immunity and witness protection. We didn't question Holt too closely about what he did in the Congo and who with, but he did tell us that he was with five others and only three of them were left, and he also mentioned you were pushing a vendetta against him. Vendetta. His word.

'Now, Mendes contacted us a few days ago, and he, too, said he had some information for us on the Congo. He specifically took Holt's name and said he was aware Holt was informing on Al Qaeda and he had additional information.'

'So talk to him. Why are you wasting my time?'

'He'll only talk to you.'

'And if I refuse?'

'We could make you talk to him.'

He shifts on his feet when Zeb gazes at him, his eyes cold, boring holes through Isakson, making the ridiculousness of Isakson's comment obvious.

'We need your help,' Isakson repeats. 'Mendes might have more intel, and we can't pass up any opportunity to get more on Al Qaeda.'

'Looks like it was pretty easy for you to ignore the mass rape and killing of women and children in the Congo. Or didn't your new best friend, Holt, tell you what he was up to over there? Maybe you didn't even ask.'

Isakson flushes deeply. 'That was not my call. Way above my pay grade. You should know how these things work.'

Zeb looks at him contemptuously. 'That rationalization makes you sleep better at night?'

A vein beats rapidly on Isakson's forehead as he struggles to control himself. After a long silence he takes a deep breath. 'Whether I do is not your concern. Will you speak to Mendes?'

'Set it up.'

Isakson shows Zeb out. 'Major,' he calls out as Zeb steps out.

Zeb pauses, doesn't turn.

'We want you to get all the intel you can from him, not

kill him. We would be most upset if anything happened to Mendes during your meeting.'

Zeb continues without a word.

'I don't like it,' says Broker, when Zeb updates him. 'The timing is too coincidental. Let's face it; they have absolutely no love for you. If anything happened to you, they wouldn't shed any tears. What's stopping Holt from taking you out with a long gun as you meet Mendes?'

'I'm going to meet him,' and on that Zeb hangs up.

They meet at a crowded café near Times Square, late evening. Mendes's choice. Mendes has specifically requested that Zeb meet him alone and that Zeb be dressed in tight clothes so that he can conceal no weapons.

Zeb is aware that Isakson has posted undercover agents around the café. He wanted Zeb to wear a wire, but Zeb flatly refused. Zeb is seated with his back to the wall, thick walls, enough to stop even a Barrett M107 shot.

Mendes is thinner than portrayed in the agency files. Disheveled. Greasy hair and beard, he's not exactly a role model for personal hygiene products. His eyes dart around, meeting Zeb's only briefly.

'It's *you* who's after us.'

Zeb doesn't say anything. Studies him, watches his hands tremble. Zeb's radar is not pinging, so he thinks Mendes has come alone. He's wearing a jacket that could conceal a gun, but that doesn't bother Zeb.

'Holt mentioned that you killed Con, Brink...I didn't see the bodies. Jones and I had left earlier.

'We were six. The world was ours.' He laughs harshly. 'Now look where we are. Three of us left, hunted by you. Hunted by just one man, with no support from anyone. Who are you, man?'

He looks around. 'I should kill you. Holt said whoever sees you should shoot you on the spot.'

Zeb can sense the undercover agents inching closer. Isakson was bound to be using parabolic mics to pick up their conversation, and Mendes's last utterance would have sent the agents to highest alert.

Mendes turns back to Zeb. 'Now that bastard has become an FBI informer, I hear. He's safe and protected, but not Jones or I. We were with him. We both know as much as him, if not more. We also want to be protected from a madman like you and whoever else is out there.'

'If I'm mad, what does that make you? And why ask for me? You could have had this conversation with the FBI, the NYPD, anyone.' Zeb's eyes bore holes in him.

'I didn't think the cops or anyone else would take me seriously. I wasn't sure if I could trust them either; hence I told them I would talk only to you. I guess your coming shows how badly they want my information.'

'If they wanted your intel that badly, they would've met you. There wasn't any need for going through me. Unless it was to set me up.'

Mendes meets his eyes briefly and looks away. 'I have my reasons. As for setting you up – that's the risk you willingly took.'

He pauses reflectively. 'Once we went to Somalia, we were like animals. That country changed us. Holt changed us. Maybe we wanted to change. I was different before the Congo. I believed in good, in rightness, in justice. But there...' He trails off.

He smiles crookedly, still not meeting Zeb's eyes. 'What we did there...it doesn't leave you.'

'You telling me you got a taste for raping and killing girls now?' Zeb asks.

Mendes stills his nervous twitching and goes white. He finally looks at Zeb. 'It sits on your shoulder. Always. And it eats away at you.'

'You looking for sympathy and forgiveness?'

Mendes stares at Zeb. Zeb is sprawled, relaxed. And ready.

'Tell your friends in the FBI that I have more information than Holt has, to close down cells. Holt just gave the orders. I and the others did all the dirty work and got up-close and personal with the locals and know better than Holt, what the Al Qaeda are doing there. I know names, numbers, cells, locations, the way they work...a shit load more than what Holt knows and is feeding them. In return I want immunity. I want you to set this up for me.'

'And why do you think I give a shit about what you want? I want you. Every one of you and mostly Holt. Why the fuck should I play matchmaker for you when I would rather plug you dead?'

'Then I'm wasting my time with you. And as for killing me, you won't. You see, you're my insurance policy now. If you kill me, or I die for whatever reason, the FBI will come down on you faster than a ton of bricks.' He smiles coldly, the nervous twitching all gone.

He stands up, looking down at Zeb, who is still sprawled in his seat. 'Get them to give me the same deal that they're giving Holt, or I'll go public with their dirty dealing and bring this shit crashing down on them.'

Mendes looks at him a moment, then turns around and walks out.

Zeb follows him a moment later.

Mendes stops outside the café, with Zeb a few feet behind him. New York swirls around them and goes about its business. The agents are there. Zeb can sense them.

'You know, Holt was right.' Mendes turns his head to look back at Zeb.

A woman facing Mendes screams. 'Gun! He's got a gun!'

Mendes turns smoothly towards Zeb, his right arm sliding out of his jacket, holding a gun. People dive to the pavement, taking shelter behind up-ended tables as more screams punctuate the air.

Zeb stands still. Nothing exists now but the straightening arm of Mendes with the gun at the end of it.

Isakson breaks cover from inside an anonymous car and runs towards the two of them. 'Stop. FBI. Throw down your gun.'

More FBI agents run screaming orders at the two.

Isakson sees Mendes's arm straightening, his forefinger heading to the trigger as he sights Zeb.

Zeb is still standing motionless, and only when the gun has reached Mendes's eyes does he move. All Isakson sees is a blur.

Bad time for an itch, he thinks, and the next moment the Benchmade Entourage buries itself in Mendes's throat.

Isakson has been watching Zeb, screaming at him to duck, and he still could not see Zeb's arm move as he threw the knife. Isakson sprints to Mendes, stoops over his fallen body, and removes the gun from his hand. One of his agents has called the paramedics, and the other agents are holding back the crowd of people, shielding them from Mendes and dispersing them. Isakson tries to stem the flow of blood from

Mendes but can see it's in vain. Zeb's knife has severed the major arteries and major muscles in his throat.

Isakson joins Zeb, who is still standing motionless, looking dispassionately at Mendes.

'I was listening in. You didn't ask him anything about Al Qaeda, which is what I was interested in.'

'Not my problem.'

Isakson shakes his head, trying to understand what's happened. 'Craziest thing I've seen or heard. He sets out his terms and then decides to kill you. Surely he would have known there was no way he could have escaped after shooting you.'

Zeb replies drily, 'That was sorta what he wanted.'

Isakson sees the media swarm approaching and leaves to head them off. He shouts over his shoulder, 'I'm majorly pissed that you didn't ask him about his intel. For that alone I might just be tempted to feed you to the media.'

Zeb disappears into the throng.

'You did what? Killed him in Times Square, in broad daylight, in front of thousands of people?' Broker exclaims when Zeb briefs him.

'Near Times Square. In the evening. And he was drawing a gun on me. You wanted me to pray?'

'Yup, I see your point. Four down now,' Broker says gleefully.

'By the way, didn't you say Isakson was going to hand you over on a platter to the media?'

'He didn't put it quite that way, but I wouldn't put it beyond him.'

'Hold on. Let me check the news.'

Broker comes back a few minutes later. 'Nada. Not a thing about you. There is a brief story about a man being killed near Times Square and that the police are investigating it, but no details. Nothing much on cyberspace either, and I checked the usual – Twitter, Facebook, that shit. Let me do some digging and find out why Isakson had a change of heart. I doubt he has a heart, but we'll never know for sure.

'What's next?' he asks Zeb.

'Nothing's changed,' replies Zeb. 'I'll continue to paint target circles on myself.'

'Are you going back to Williamstown in the next few days?' asks Broker.

'Nope. I'm thinking of joining the Balthazars on their mountain trip. I wasn't planning to go, but if Isakson feeds me to the press, then it might be better to disappear for a short while.'

'What if Holt comes after you there?'

'I did think of that, and that's the reason I wasn't willing initially. However, if Isakson has a change of heart, then Cassandra and the Balthazars will inevitably get sucked into the media scrum, whatever happens. If Holt comes at me in the mountains, I'll deal with it. I'll be ready. I'll warn Connor, however, and leave the final decision to him.'

'Good thinking. I'll come back to you if I hear anything about Isakson's angelic act.'

Its late night when Zeb goes to the tabla school, but it's still open, and he can hear the sounds of the drums. When he pushes open the doors, he sees that the hall is empty but for his teacher. His teacher smiles widely on seeing Zeb and beckons him silently. He eyes Zeb silently as he approaches.

'This is a place to heal. Not to wage war.'

'I have known only war all my life.'

His teacher smiles. 'The tabla does not bond with those that only destroy.'

Zeb is silent. His teacher looks at him silently and then launches into the Ardha Taal Chakra. A half-beat tabla taal that starts with the smallest rhythm circle, growing one beat at a time, pulling Zeb into its ripples.

It's early morning when Zeb returns to yet another transient hotel. Broker has left him a message.

'I have news for you.'

Chapter 12

'The Director's still batting for you. Isakson was going to make a press statement releasing the details of Mendes's killing when she got wind of it. She called the FBI's Director and said that a certain Special Agent in Charge had better like cleaning toilet bowls in Idaho, because that would be the only job he'd get once she was through with him. She also said the same SAC could be booked under the Patriot Act for risking sensitive operational details. I guess she meant the media digging into your past.

'Of course, that made Isakson even madder,' continues Broker, on getting the predictable silence from Zeb.

'But nothing has changed much as far as the FBI is concerned. Holt is still their best buddy–'

Zeb interrupts him before he can continue his rant. 'I'm thinking of writing a letter to his mother describing him as a rapist. I'm sure she and he check their mail.'

Broker chuckles. 'If you do the latter, it will make him mad as a hornet, and then if you disappear into the mountains untraceable, it will make him madder. Maybe that's what you should do.

'You know, I could just hack into the FBI's systems, find out where he's put up, and you could go and get him. So simple, instead of this elaborate version of being the sacrificial lamb. Not that you're very lamblike.' Broker snorts.

'No. I want him to come out of his comfort zone and come after me.'

'Have it your way, Mr. Stubborn. When are you off to the mountains?'

'I'll speak to Connor today. They're leaving in a couple of days, and I'll join them if he's still okay with my going along.'

'I have an idea. How far away would you stay from your mother if you were very close to her?'

'I wasn't close to my mother. I don't even know who she was. Cassandra and I were orphaned just after birth.'

It's Broker's turn to be silent. This is news to even him.

'But to answer your question, if I were close to my mother, I wouldn't live much more than an hour away from her – hour and a half at most.'

'Yes, that's what I also thought,' says Broker briskly. 'And on that basis, I'm searching for houses in Williamstown which have been rented or sold in the last six months that are about two hours away from Holt's mother. Assuming that she does stay in her home.'

Zeb's impressed. 'Great thinking. Hanging out with me is paying off.'

Broker snorts. 'Hanging out with me is sure as hell giving you a sense of humor. Who would have thought?'

Zeb calls Connor and tells him about the baggage surrounding him without going into the specifics.

'I know Rory wants you to come. I'll talk to Lauren and Anne and let you know, but I think it'll be fine,' Connor answers sanguinely.

Zeb frowns at his phone. 'I'm not sure you realize the kind of danger you're putting yourself in. This isn't like anything you've ever experienced. Think of the worst peril you folks have been in, times it a million and it still won't be close.'

There's a long silence at the other end.

'You there?' Zeb asks.

Connor chuckles. 'Yeah. I'm recovering. I didn't know you had so many words in you. And about the danger, peril, all that stuff – I still want you to come. However, I *will* talk to Lauren and get back to you.'

Zeb tells Cassandra everything. She makes no comment and leaves it to Connor to make the final call. She had already pieced together most of the story from Clare's comments to her.

Zeb has wanted to get kitted out for some time, and now is as good a time as ever. He has been getting his kit from a supplier that the agency uses and has been vetted by Broker. This time he decides to go to Bunk Talbot for a change.

Talbot's gun shop is surrounded by the usual badasses hanging around, giving the stare to anyone who steps into their territory.

Zeb's bemused when he sees them. There must be a book on eBay, *'Tude for Badasses* the way all of them give off the same vibe, he thinks. Most of them will not live out a year, but hey, attitude is king.

'You again. I was wondering when you'd show up. I got nothing for you – same as before,' grunts Talbot on spotting Zeb.

'Sniper rifles, handguns and knives are what I'm after,' replies Zeb.

'Doing business with me now so that I pass some info? That dog won't hunt, pal.'

'I'm here to buy. If you won't sell, then I'm wasting my time.'

Talbot stares at Zeb and wordlessly puts out a hand.

Zeb slaps his shopping list in his palm. Talbot looks at it for a moment and goes to the back of his shop. He returns with a clanking duffel bag and drops it in front of Zeb.

Zeb is looking out of the window at the men on the street.

'Clones,' he mutters.

'That they are. They wouldn't last a day in 'Stan or Iraq.'

'Any of them tried holding you up?'

'Tried. I'm still here. They aren't,' replies Talbot impassively.

Zeb opens the duffel and inspects the weapons. An AWM sniper rifle, a couple of sniper scopes, a few Predator knives, and three Sig Sauer handguns. Ammunition neatly boxed up. Talbot may be servicing the wrong people, but he has the right goods. Something makes Zeb look up.

There is a fourth Sig. Talbot is pointing it squarely at Zeb.

Zeb can sense two people entering the store and blocking the exit.

'Last time you asked me to tell Holt that you're hunting him. You came to me just because I trained with him. I sell guns. Weapons. I don't care who I sell to. However, I do not knowingly sell to people who wage war on women and children. And I didn't sell to Holt. Never did. And I didn't tell him about your visit. Never *brokered* information,' Talbot spits, letting Zeb know that he knows about Broker.

He puts down the gun and slides it butt-first to Zeb. The tension escapes the room like air from a pricked balloon.

Zeb removes his hands from inside the duffel bag. His right holding a fully loaded Sig aimed at Talbot through the bag. He places it alongside Talbot's gun, looking straight at him.

Talbot cracks the slightest smile, realizing that he would have been dead if he had pulled the trigger. He sees now why his Seal buddies told him not to rub Zeb the wrong way.

Zeb leaves with the duffel bag. Every once in a while someone surprises him.

There's another surprise waiting for him when Connor calls him later.

'Are you sure? Are you aware of what you might get into?'

'Moneybags put it eloquently, the charms of taking a dump

in the mountains fade after some time, so if you invite trouble, then it'll liven things up and I'll have stories to tell at the water cooler.'

'This is not some macho game. You all could end up dead,' Zeb tells him bluntly.

'You leave that to us, Zeb, just be there.' There is a smile in Connor's voice as he hangs up.

Broker is uncharacteristically supportive of Connor's decision. Zeb expects him to launch a fusillade at weekend warriors, but he delivers a limp, 'Their life, their death,' instead. Maybe Broker is mellowing with age. Maybe hell has frozen over.

Zeb goes to the shooting range run by Bear and Chloe to center the AWM and get used to it. He then packs his armory, ready for an early start the next day. He leaves a message for Broker to let him know if there is any media coverage on him.

Zeb is going separately and a day later than the others deliberately. As he drives out of the city early the next day, the urban frenzy of the city gives way to I-87, and time slows down.

'Well, hurry up; there are bears to be shot and fish to be caught,' Connor says impatiently when he calls and finds that Zeb has left just an hour back.

'Bear shooting? I don't think so.' Zeb hears Rory protesting in the background.

It's well past noon when Zeb reaches their camp. It's in one of the remotest parts of the Catskill Mountains, in the West Kill Mountain Wilderness Area. He parks his Jeep alongside theirs in a parking lot off Route 28 and then hikes a couple of miles to the coordinates given to him by Connor.

Their camp is in the open, tents put up by Connor and the women, about three hundred yards from thick woods. Zeb drifts through the woods, effortlessly becoming one with the foliage, and watches the camp for a long time, getting used to the sounds of the woods and the mountains.

He can see Rory playing with a Frisbee with Connor, and can see shadows moving in the tents. Something feels wrong, and he stays where he is, trying to figure it out. Finally he gives up. His radar isn't pinging, so he doesn't think there's any danger.

He steps into the open and walks to the tents, his hands close to his sides.

Rory spots him, gives a whoop, and rushes toward him.

Zeb catches Rory and gives him a quick hug with his left hand, then stops suddenly, looking beyond Rory.

Chapter 13

From behind the tents emerge Connor puffing away contentedly on his foul-smelling pipe, Lauren, Anne, Cassandra, and Anne's boyfriend.

But that's not what makes Zeb stop.

Standing farther behind them, spread out, are Broker, Bear and Chloe.

'You really didn't think we would let you have all the fun yourself, did you?' rumbles Broker.

Bear holds his hands up. 'Not my idea. Connor and this dude, their danged idea. Blame them.'

Zeb walks silently to the tents and finds one empty, erected for him by Bear and Broker, and places his stuff within and walks out.

'Are you mad at us, Zeb? Dad thought this was the best way to get all of us together,' Rory asks.

Zeb's hard face softens the slightest bit. 'Nope. I'm okay. I was just surprised to see these guys here. To Bear, roughing it is staying at a Motel 6 instead of a Hyatt.'

'I like him. He plays ball with me and is helping me with my pitching.'

'Yes,' agrees Zeb, 'he's a nice guy. But just make sure you sleep far away from him. He snores like a jet engine.'

It's dusk when they finish playing. Broker has gone hunting since Connor's plan was to let Rory experience living close to nature. Bear goes foraging for firewood, with Rory skipping excitedly beside him, while Zeb clears a large patch of grass for the fire. He arranges the firewood while Bear digs out loose soil to put the fire out later in the evening.

When Broker returns with two freshly skinned rabbits, everybody is lounging around a roaring fire.

'As I thought. I do all the heavy lifting, and you guys watch the grass grow.' He unslings the rabbits and puts them over the fire on a spit he makes expertly.

'You guys have made all of us redundant.' Connor laughs. 'We might as well just sit back and have you take care of us.'

'Did you guys serve together?' asks Mark. Zeb has met Moneybags a few times, but it's only here and now that he learns his actual name.

'Nope. Broker and Zeb were in Somalia at the same time and then were together in various other places. Zeb and I were in

Afghanistan. Broker and I hooked up once I left the service.' Bear ladles food into their plates as he replies to Mark.

'And is your name really Bear?'

'Well, I prefer Bear to my real name.' He grins.

'Someone who has faced death more than once shouldn't be afraid of revealing his real name,' teases Mark.

Bear is busy eating when he realizes everyone is looking at him. Broker and Chloe are grinning.

'It's Bozo.' He smiles sheepishly and buries his face in his hands as they all laugh.

Connor knocks his pipe out and refills it. 'Before you came here, I was telling Bear, Broker and Chloe about my exposé on mining and the stories I'm writing,' he says to Zeb. 'I've received more anonymous threats, and I reported them all to the NYPD. Not that they're going to do jack shit about it.' He snorts. 'I don't know if you read the first of my stories that appeared last week. This week's story will be in tomorrow's newspaper. Once we return, I expect to get proof of Hardinger's involvement, and then the fur will fly.'

'I've been busy,' Zeb says, 'but you should get some protection for yourself, Lauren, and Rory if you think these threats have a bite.'

'What we told him,' chimes in Broker.

'I'll think about it,' replies Connor. 'I've been in hairier situations before and didn't feel like I needed protection.'

Zeb adds some wood to the fire. 'If Hardinger is as involved as you claim, then he has everything to lose, and if he's involved in child labor in Africa, then going after you will be like swatting a fly – no offense.'

'I'll consider it when I see what proof I get from my sources.'

In the distance an owl hoots, followed by a replying hoot closer to them.

Zeb's head snaps up, listening.

The owls hoot again.

He rises smoothly, fluidly, and scrutinizes the forest. Everyone falls silent and looks at him askance.

Finally, he turns to Broker. 'Who've you told about this trip?'

'I might have let it slip to a couple of folks.' Broker is unabashed.

'Who?'

'Bwana and Roger.'

Zeb gazes at him for a long while and then walks into the darkness.

Rory is confused. 'Is Zeb leaving?'

'Nope.' Broker laughs. 'He's going to meet some friends of ours.'

Lauren is astonished. 'You mean those owl hoots were some guys Zeb knows? He recognized them? Out here? In the middle of nowhere?'

Broker nods. 'Once Connor told me about this camping trip and Zeb's warning to all of you, I called a few friends of ours. Two of them were going to be camping in the Catskills too and said they'd hang close to us. We all have call signs for one another. It's not difficult to make out who's who based on the call sign.'

Connor smiles with quiet satisfaction and puffs away at his pipe. 'I bet those camping plans of theirs got made on the fly. Do they know Bear and Chloe too?'

Broker nods. 'We work in a small circle. We all know one another.'

'I don't understand,' Anne interjects. 'Why would those two men drop whatever they're doing and come charging out here just because you told them about Zeb and his problems?'

Broker doesn't answer, and Chloe fills the silence. 'There are people who owe a lot to Zeb. Two of them are by this campfire. Two more are out there.'

'Zeb is a big part of our lives. Big. When he's in trouble, we come running,' adds Bear.

'But don't mention that to him. He'd go purple batshit.' Broker chuckles.

In the woods, Zeb walks towards the sounds of the first owl hoot and waits.

Presently a figure appears from the dark, an ebony shadow amongst other shadows. They hug silently.

'Long time. You look like crap.' Bwana's smile gleams in the dark. Zeb feels Roger's presence behind him and turns around to face both. He bumps fists with Roger.

'Why?' he asks.

'Why not?' drawls Roger. 'We were going fishing anyway. Fishing here is just as good.'

'Better,' counters Bwana, 'especially if Rog does the hard work.'

'Better,' agrees Roger, 'but we draw straws on the work.'

'So what shit is stuck to your shoes now?'

Zeb starts from Luvungi.

'Hell, I've never understood this pussyfooting from you. Seen it many times. If I was you, I would just get Broker to dig out his address, storm it, and stick a knife in him. Come to think of it, I might just do it myself,' Bwana says.

Roger chews a stem of grass. 'Do you think this dude will really come over here with an army?'

'Nope. As long as he's feeding the FBI, he's secure. I don't think he'll do anything to jeopardize his witness protection. But I have to be prepared for anything.'

Zeb works out attack and defense plans with them in case Holt arrives. On his return to the camp, he halts near the edge of the woods and notes the layout of the tents. The central tents are those of the Balthazars, Anne and Mark, and Cassandra, while the outer ones circling them are those of Broker, Bear and Chloe, and Zeb.

As he steps soundlessly into the camp, a shape detaches itself from the ground and goes into a tent. Bear settles to sleep as Zeb takes over the watch. Arrangements made in different lifetimes in far dusty lands, still continuing wordlessly today.

The next day they go hiking on Devil's Path, with Broker leading, Bear and Chloe in the middle, and Rory and Zeb in the rear. Rory's inquisitiveness fills the vast stillness of the mountains. They fall back from the main group as he darts away from the trail to look at whatever interests him.

They resume their hike when he joins Zeb, his pockets full of stones of different colors for his collection.

'Zeb, did you get in fights in school?'

'Some.'

'Did you win them all?'

'Nope. I lost most of them.'

Rory's mouth turns into an O. 'I can't believe that. I was thinking you would have whupped everyone's asses.'

'Nope. Mine got whupped most of the time.'

'Is that why you got in the army? To learn how to fight?'

Zeb's face twitches. 'No. I joined the army because I wanted to. I fit in there. I used to lose fights in school because I didn't learn to walk away from them. Not every fight should be fought.'

'My friends tell me I'm a wimp if I don't fight.'

'Maybe they're not such good friends of yours if they tell

you that. If anyone picks on you, you should report them to your teacher, not get into fights.'

Rory rolls his eyes. 'Zeb, you sound just like Mom. I bet you had loads of friends in school. I like Broker and Bear. They treat me like a grown-up.'

Zeb walks in silence for a long while. 'I didn't have any friends in school. It didn't bother me. I was my own friend.'

'I don't have any in school either,' Rory says very softly. 'I have just three now. Broker, Bear and you.'

Zeb looks down at him. 'Three is enough. It's not how many friends you have but how important you are to them.'

They are still some distance away from the main group, and when Lauren turns to look back at them, she stumbles and bumps into Connor. He, too, looks back and sees Rory holding hands with Zeb.

His look of utter amazement makes the others look back too. 'Well, I'll be damned,' Mark exclaims. 'I never thought I would see Zeb holding anyone's hand, much less a little boy's!'

Broker looks at Bear and shrugs. They long ago stopped being amazed by whatever Zeb does.

As they approach the Buck's Ridge lookout, a couple of rabbits dart across the trail. Two rifles greet them, just a fraction of a second apart.

'Lunch.' Broker sighs. He and Bear pick up their kills, stuff them in sacks, and sling them over their shoulders.

'Holy shit,' whispers Mark to Anne. 'That was some shooting. Rifle across back, to hand, and firing before I even noticed the rabbits. I'm glad these guys are on our side.' He looks back and whispers, 'Zeb didn't even unlimber. I'm surprised.'

'He doesn't need to when these guys are around,' Anne replies dryly.

A bird call rings out in the distance. Only Zeb and Bear notice Broker tensing slightly and then relaxing when another call answers.

Bwana and Roger are on either side of them, keeping them in sight but out of sight themselves.

They resume their hike after their lunch. The sheer scale of the wilderness has brought their small talk to a minimum. Anne's abrasiveness with Zeb has disappeared. Or maybe it's just a lull before she starts again. Mark has coped very well in the wilderness despite his city-boy ways. Maybe the wilderness is not all that different to the stock market.

It's late evening by the time they return to camp. A hot dinner revives them, and Connor – after lighting his pipe, which, according to him, keeps the wild animals at bay – recounts stories from his career as a reporter.

Broker, no mean raconteur himself, joins in telling stories of past campaigns.

Lauren, Anne, Rory and Mark have led urban lives and haven't had any contact with the likes of Zeb and his friends. Their lives are fascinating to them.

'No, most campaign days are one of endless routine and monotony. The danger, the action, is all over in a few minutes usually,' replies Broker in response to a question from Anne.

'Have you guys lost any friends?' Rory asks.

'Yup,' comes the terse response.

Silence descends.

'What was your most dangerous moment?' Rory again.

'Well...'

Bear starts grinning and then guffawing.

Rory is puzzled, and he's not the only one. 'What?'

Broker looks sheepish. 'There was this time we parachuted into bad country. I won't name the country because the operation is still classified.

'So we had done a HALO jump very late at night and landed in enemy territory. We were then supposed to march about ten clicks to a specific village, which housed a lot of badasses, photograph those badasses as they were doing their bad stuff, and then apprehend them.'

'Sounds like a stupid assignment. Why not just finish them?' mutters Mark.

'Hey, who said the top brass running the army were the brightest sparks? But ours was not to question why, so like good little soldiers, we marched the ten clicks to the village.

'We reached it early in the morning, but it was still dark, so we couldn't make out anything, just lots of foliage and rocks. However, our compasses told us we had arrived, so we stopped.

'We decided to hunker down for the rest of the night and begin our surveillance in broad daylight. There were five of us in that team.' He gestures toward Zeb. 'He was there too.

'I settled in a small ditch, which was recently dug – I could smell the fresh earth. I cut some brush and pulled it over me and settled down to sleep with one of the others keeping watch.

'When I woke up, it was raining. It was daylight, and I could feel movement around me. I was still groggy from the previous night...remember I was an intelligence guy and not as battle hardened as these other guys. I opened my eyes a little to have a look at who or what was moving around.'

He pauses to poke a few sticks in the fire, and everyone leans forward in anticipation.

'I was shocked to find that it was a goat pissing on me!'

He is rewarded with roars of laughter. He waits for it to die down and then lifts his hand to silence them.

'I heard voices around me, and after listening carefully, I made out that somehow we had stumbled into the middle of a grazing area of the hostiles we were after. I tried to look around for where the rest of my team was but couldn't see anyone. Occasionally I saw a couple of hostiles walk past my hideout, fully armed. If they had bothered to look down, they would have seen me, and I would have had more holes than a sieve.

'All day long goats pissed on me, even dumped on me. Then, in the evening, to my horror, one of the goats started munching on the brush covering me like it was dinner at the Carnegie Deli.

'It was pulling it away and then eating it. I pulled the brush back over me as stealthily as possible, and the goat pulled it right back again. Tug-of-war between goat and Broker, smack in the middle of hostile country.

'I got desperate because I was practically exposed. I lifted my head a little and looked around. A few hostiles, but none too close to me, and none looking in my direction. I took my rifle and smacked the goat a good one in the breadbasket.

'The goat jumped up and ran away, but that action got noticed by one of the hostiles, and he approached me. I could see him from the corner of my eyes.

'This is it. I wrote a long letter to Mama in my head and told her that when we met in heaven, she could smack me all she wanted for kissing seven-year-old Peggy in the kitchen.

'And by the way, I was seven too when that happened, so stop those dirty thoughts right now!'

Rory is rolling around in laughter by now, and the rest of them are close to following him.

'But as luck would have it, that damned goat took it in his mind to charge that guy. He just put his head down and butted him, throwing him on his ass. That guy forgot about investigating my ditch and started wrestling with the goat.

'When night fell and those guys were asleep, I crawled out and crept away. My team was waiting for me not far from these hostiles, and we regrouped.

'That goat saved my life! From that day, I decided I'll let any goat pee all over me as much as he wants.'

That sets off Rory laughing again.

When he has calmed down, he asks, 'Where were Zeb and the rest of your team?'

'What I asked! Zeb had been sent scouting, so he was nowhere near the camp. The rest of our team was scattered in similar ditches, but I was the only one smack dab in the middle of the hostiles. When they realized where we were, it was too late to warn me.'

A night owl calls in the distance a few times as Broker feeds more wood in the fire.

'But never drink goat's piss. Not a pleasant taste.'

Mark chuckles. 'I guess when you guys have lived in the rough, you have to eat and drink all kinds of stuff, don't you?'

Before Broker can reply, a, 'Halloo the camp,' rings out, and two trappers step into the firelight.

'Hi, guys, pretty late to be wandering around,' Connor greets them.

'Nope, this is the right time for us guys, as we lay our traps and check on them,' replies the taller of the two, glancing around, adding, 'Howdy, ma'am,' in the women's direction.

'Care for some coffee?' Connor offers. He realizes that Bear and Chloe are hanging back, nearly shrouded in darkness, while there is no sign of Zeb. Broker is sitting easy and relaxed by the fire, with Rory next to him.

'No, sir, thanks for asking. We were tramping across to check our traps when we spotted your fire. There's a big black bear around here with cubs. Thought we should warn you.'

'Much appreciated. Bear meat's not my favorite, but we'll keep that in mind,' replies Broker.

Zeb is with Bwana. He slipped away once he heard the owl hoots.

'Just two trappers, harmless enough. I was tracking them for some time and overheard some snippets of conversation.

There is a bear in the vicinity. I overheard them and also spotted some tracks.'

'You need any rations? Anything?'

'We're good, man. Fishing and having a great time.'

Zeb pats him on the back and returns to camp.

'There you are,' Connor says, pointing his pipe at him.

'All okay?' Bear murmurs as Zeb walks past him.

Zeb nods imperceptibly.

Rain pours down late that night, waking Lauren up. She pokes her head out of the tent to see the camp silent and lit by the dim light of the lanterns within the tents. As she scans the trees, something catches the corner of her eye.

A figure is standing at the edge of the tents, motionless. She stares hard through the rain, trying to see who it is.

It's Zeb.

He has his face raised to the rain, standing motionless as it beats down on him. She is about to call out when Connor places his hand on her shoulder.

'Leave him be.'

She takes one last look at him, a tall solitary figure unmoving, the rain washing down on him.

The ground is soggy the next day, but the water has drained away, something Connor is very proud of since he chose the campsite. Lauren refrains from mentioning that Broker and Bear nudged him to this site.

Bear has returned from scouting and mentions bear tracks not far from their site, and when they set out on a hike, they detour to show Rory the tracks.

Broker whistles when he sees them. He kneels down, motioning Rory to do the same, and points out the bear's tracks to him, as well as two other sets of tracks a little to the side.

'Cubs,' he says.

Zeb is looking over his shoulder at the three sets of tracks. He nudges Broker, who rises and pulls Rory to his feet.

'Let's get back to our hike.' He leads the way back to their trail.

Lauren and Anne catch up with Zeb. 'What's the hurry? It would have been great to follow those tracks and show Rory the bears.'

'It's better if the bears find us than us go looking for them, ma'am,' he replies. 'Besides, mama bear is large – bigger than

I've seen in a long time.'

They meet the trappers halfway through their trek and stop to have coffee with them.

'I would be extra careful if I was you.' The taller of the two looks at Broker. 'There's one more bear in the vicinity, a male, who has gone through some camps, ripped some tents, and stolen food. Those cubs might be his.'

'We'll keep a watch.' Broker nods in thanks.

'We seem to be surrounded by bears,' Cassandra says once they resume their hike.

'Yup, and we have one along with us, too!' Rory guffaws, pointing to Bear.

* * *

It's close to dusk when they come across it.

They're in a small clearing surrounded by thick brush and woods, and Broker is doing what he does best, spinning yarns and entertaining them. Zeb is bringing up the rear, and as Rory doubles up in laughter, he spins around, looks at Zeb, and screams.

Lauren and Anne look back too and join the chorus of yells. Zeb has felt its presence long before the others spotted it but didn't sense any danger radiating from it. He has been subtly falling behind the group to distance himself from them and was planning to lead it away before anyone spotted it.

He turns around slowly and faces the largest bear he has ever seen, nearly ten feet away and close to six hundred and fifty pounds. The bear has crept up on them silently on all fours and is looking directly at Zeb, with its ears back.

'Broker,' he calls out softly.

'Gotcha. Come on, folks. Let's move away and go back to our site. Zeb will deal with this critter.'

They move slowly with the occasional glance back, and when they're out of the clearing and back into the woods, they stop to look back.

Zeb moves his eyes away from the bear and takes a step back. The bear shuffles forward, barking as it does so.

Zeb stands still.

And the bear charges.

Over in the woods Connor cups his hand over Rory's mouth as they all watch the bear rushing at an unbelievable speed, come to a few feet from Zeb, break away at the last moment and go past him.

'Holy shit, I didn't think they could move so fast. How the hell is he standing there so calmly?' Connor says under his breath.

Zeb turns to face the bear, which is now walking slowly around, keeping him in sight. The bear pauses, staring directly at Zeb, popping its jaws, and then charges again, swerves again when it's just a couple of feet away, and turns around as it goes past. The bear charges again without any warning and comes to a stop a foot away, black muscle and fury staring directly at Zeb.

Connor can hear the bear barking right in Zeb's face, the rage and spittle washing over him, yet Zeb stands his ground. He can see Zeb's lips move, but they're too far away to hear him. The bear continues looking at Zeb directly for long moments, its muscles bunched, and then it rises on its hind legs, sniffing at Zeb. It nudges Zeb with its nose, smelling him all over, falls back to all fours, walks around him, and then ambles into the woods as noiselessly as it had come.

Connor lets out a long breath he didn't know he had held and looks around to the others.

Broker, Bear and Chloe are laughing quietly at something.

'You guys weren't even watching?'

'Nothing to see. We knew it wouldn't be hurt. The bear, I mean.' Broker chuckles.

Rory rushes towards Zeb excitedly and peppers him with questions about the bear. Connor can see that this bear encounter will be the highlight of the trip for Rory.

'Mom, Zeb says he wasn't scared when the bear came so close to him. How cool is that?'

Anne replies, 'We know, dear. And Zeb can walk on water too.'

Broker's rumbling laugh echoes in the woods as they make their way back to the campsite, while Bear slips off to warn Bwana and Roger about the black bear.

Over the campfire, Anne looks at Zeb. 'Have you never been scared?'

Zeb shrugs.

Bear answers for him. 'Everyone gets scared. Everyone. We used to get shit scared on our missions. Still do sometimes. Zeb is different. He hasn't...' He breaks off and yelps when Chloe accidentally pours hot coffee over his hand.

Anne forgets her question as she rushes to pour cold water

over the injured extremity and misses the warning glances that pass from Broker to Chloe and Bear.

But Connor doesn't. *Hmm, this needs investigating,* he thinks and makes a mental note to ask Cassandra what that was all about.

Chapter 14

'I got them,' Connor shouts at Zeb on the phone as they are all driving back the next day, back to the city and urban frenzy.

'Those emails that incriminate Hardinger? They got sent to my office yesterday and are with our expensive lawyers. I haven't seen them yet, but my editor says they're explosive, and hence the discussions with the suits. It's game on now, baby.'

Over Connor's excitement, Zeb can hear Lauren's anxious voice, 'Now the pressure on you and us will really start.'

'Let it. This is what I do for a living, and I love it,' replies Connor impatiently.

'Zeb, can you guys – Broker, Bear, and Chloe – come over in a day or two? I'd like your opinions on what can be done to deal with the threats and nuisance once the story hits.'

'Okay.'

Broker calls minutes later. 'Did you get the Connor invite?'

'Yup.'

'Should we get involved?'

'I am involved because they're Cassandra's neighbors.'

'Then we're involved, too. And Roger and Bwana say they'd like to help kill weeds in this garden.'

* * *

Before departing from the mountains, Broker and Bear met with Bwana and Roger in the woods. Bwana had been his usual subtle self.

'Pond scum belongs in the pond. Tell Zeb I'll be happy to help.'

'Behind me,' Roger had broken in.

'When are you planning to meet Connor?' Broker asks Zeb.

'Whenever he calls. I don't have anything on my plate right now.'

As Connor drives, he looks at Cassandra in the mirror.

'Cass, what's it that Bear was going to say before Chloe burned his hand? I know she did it deliberately.'

Cassandra looks at him and then away. 'I wouldn't know.'

Connor lets the silence build, hoping it will get her talking, but she has nothing further to say.

He smiles, remembering that she lived and worked in Washington and knows how to keep a secret.

Zeb checks into a seedy hotel in Harlem, returns his Jeep, and then visits his apartment in Jackson Heights to check it out. His fingerprint, laid across the bottom of the door and jamb is still there, as is a thin film of dust in a specific pattern across the side.

He steps in, moves to the right, and stands still to feel the sound and smell of his apartment, finds nothing out of the ordinary, and goes to his arms cache. It's time to redistribute it across the city, considering that he'll be spending a lot of time in hotels till he sorts out the Holt issue.

He's always used a network of storage boxes in any city he lives in and already has such a network here, but he wants to supplement it.

It's late in the evening when he heads back to his hotel after topping up his stores. He's thinking over ways to get Holt to emerge when Connor calls him and suggests they meet the next day.

* * *

'Wow, this place is bursting at the seams with hard cases,' Connor jokes, referring to Zeb, Bear, Chloe and Broker at his place.

Connor hands over a sheaf of papers to Zeb. 'They were delivered here when we got back. The suits have approved publishing, and now it's down to me to write the mother of all stories.'

The papers were emails between RH and someone named Vince Spadea – several of them over more than a year.

'RH is the Senator obviously; Spadea was his head of security in Africa at that time, responsible for the security of all Alchemy's African businesses.'

Zeb reads the emails, passing each page to the others once he's through with them. In one mail Spadea complains that there isn't enough labor to staff the mines, to which RH replied, 'Who said the laborers have to be adults? Pay the natives and get kids, old people, anyone. I don't care.'

In another email Spadea replied, 'Boss, we're going into dangerous territory. We can't use kids. There's no more labor to be recruited. We just have to accept reduced output.'

To which RH came back, 'Fuck that shit. Minerals are at an all-time high. We need labor, and kids can get the rocks out as well as anyone. Let Joop handle it.'

'Boss, getting Joop in is going wild.'

'So? We're in the jungle, in case you forgot. Wild is normal.'
Another thread of mails starts from Spadea.
'The natives are getting restless. One of the children working in the mines died.'
'Use Joop. He'll know what to do.'
'That's a last-ditch option. Are you sure?'
'Yes, I am fucking sure.'
'Chief, we have to be careful. The company is much more visible because of your public profile; we can't go around doing shit like this.'
'Listen, asshole, I pay you to manage security not to be my conscience or my PR agent. Joop knows how to deal with the natives. Let him. You just make sure the work continues.'

Zeb finishes reading all the papers, which contain many more emails in a similar vein, hands them across to the others and sits watching out of the window.

Broker looks at Connor. 'These are genuine?'

'All verified, authenticated by some of the best cryptos in the country, guys who analyze IP addresses, that kind of stuff.'

'Well, hell, we just lost a Senator, then.'

Connor notes Chloe's troubled expression. 'Something bothering you?'

'How is it that he wrote all this so openly? Surely he isn't that stupid?'

'He isn't. He's one of the smartest people on the planet. However, his blind side is that his wealth and power make him believe he's untouchable, and it's gone to his head. Power makes people do stupid things and behave as if they're bulletproof.'

Anne, who has joined them, looks shaken. 'This is so vile... so monstrous. It makes me feel sick that he can hold political office and go about his business while those he's affected have no future or are dead.' She sniffs and scrubs a tear away.

'What will happen in all probability is someone from his office will lean on your editors, hush this up, and his life will continue on its merry way. Either that or he'll denigrate your credibility, your sources – everything to discredit this story. You know it's happened before.'

'Won't happen this time. For one, the NYT is not known for buckling under pressure. For another, this email trail is fully authenticated and verified by all kinds of technology specialists. There is absolutely no way Hardinger can deny he sent those mails. And finally, if the NYT does give in to pressure, then I'll publish the story on the Internet. It'll go viral and in many ways be more powerful than traditional publishing.'

He passes another sheaf of papers to Zeb. 'This is as much of the story I've written so far. It still needs some editing and some tweaks, but is almost ready to go to press.'

Zeb speed-reads through the story and finds it a hard-hitting exposé of the mining industry in Africa with a special focus on Alchemy. Connor has neatly laid out Alchemy's activities without resorting to emotion, letting the facts and the photographs tell their own story. The story is backed up by interviews, statistics and the damning email trail. Connor has also interviewed the specialists who have verified the emails.

Connor hands over a bunch of photographs. 'These are going with the story. Not all of them will be printed. Most of them will go on the online edition.'

In several photographs, Connor has circled key characters and described their relationship to Hardinger and their role in Alchemy.

Broker takes some of the photographs and starts going through them and grabs the rest of the photographs that Zeb tosses over. Zeb goes to the windows and looks out, suddenly wondering what he's doing here. He's pretty sure Connor got them together so that he can have a sounding board and at the same time has some heavies around him to reassure Lauren and Anne.

The more time he spends here, the more time Holt gets to secure his witness protection status with the FBI or escape from the country.

He senses the sudden stillness behind him before he turns around.

Broker is staring hard at a photograph, and the rest are looking at Broker's face.

Zeb strides across to him, and Broker hands him the photograph.

It's a bunch of people gathered around Hardinger, all of them smiling or laughing as if Hardinger had cracked the funniest of jokes. There's Hardinger's head of security, Spadea, neatly ovalled by Connor, various security guards, and mining personnel. The photograph was taken at one of the mines, and Zeb can see the equipment in the background, the Kleig lights standing sentinel over them all.

None of those interest Zeb after he gives them a cursory glance. It's the figure in the corner of the photograph who is shielding his face from the camera, unsuccessfully, who has his attention.

Carsten Holt.

Chapter 15

Connor sees his fingers whiten on the photograph, then relax, and curious, he steps across to look at the snap himself. 'What's it that has got you guys in a tizzy?'

'Who's that guy?' Broker asks.

'That? That's Joop.'

Broker and Bear look at Zeb, while Connor, Lauren and Anne look increasingly puzzled.

'Someone you know?'

'Yup.'

'Connected to whatever you're doing now?'

No answer.

Zeb is still, yet Connor can sense something powerful swirling inside. 'Zeb?'

Zeb tells him.

The story sounds grimmer when told in the middle of Manhattan, the background sounds of New York present though muted, with an uninflected voice-over by Zeb. Lauren disappears during his narration, and they can distantly hear sounds of her throwing up.

Zeb resumes when she returns, and the silence and the darkness in the apartment grows deeper. Connor lets out a long, loud breath when he's finished and paces around the apartment, saying nothing. 'So all this while...' He begins and then stops.

'You mean to say this guy and the others...' He has no words. 'Oh, fuck it,' he finally says and pours himself a triple scotch. He offers the bottle to the others, then replaces it when all of them decline.

He composes himself and asks Zeb, 'So this guy is here in New York? And being protected by the FBI?'

Zeb nods.

'And you know where he is?'

'We think we know where he could be,' says Broker.

'Just who's this guy in Hardinger's world?' he asks Connor.

'Joop is some kind of freelance Mr. Fix-It for them. He's not an Alchemy employee, and he's not a security contractor either – I wasn't able to work out how he got paid, but he was always around when Hardinger was there and was very close to the security people. I never spoke to him. He took great care to distance himself when I was there.'

Broker looks at Zeb. 'That's why we couldn't find him.'

'Now what?' asks Connor.

'Nothing,' replies Zeb, getting up and preparing to leave. Broker, Bear and Chloe start moving out along with him.

'You go ahead with your exposé, but you leave Joop or Holt, or whatever name he goes by, to us.'

'My story has wider implications now, hasn't it? Now I can also prove that Hardinger associates with monsters. And there is the FBI angle, that they're protecting this guy.'

'Sir, Hardinger will just deny that he knows this person in the photograph. He can just as easily say that the Joop he is referring to is someone else. It's not that uncommon a name in that part of the world. Don't forget that there's no record of this guy on Alchemy's payroll or the payroll of its contractors. Broker checked that out thoroughly. As for the FBI, the Patriot Act was made for them. They can do anything under the name of terrorism prevention.'

Broker smiles grimly. 'This guy is dangerous. I strongly suggest you don't involve him in your series. Leave this guy to the authorities or to us.'

'How about my going to the police or challenging the FBI with my story?' Connor asks.

'I can't advise you on what you should do, other than telling you that if I were you, I would think twice about involving Holt in this story. The police? This is beyond their jurisdiction, I'd say. The FBI might just arrest you for obstruction of justice or whatever they can think of. We tried going to them and were warned off. Whatever you do, I strongly suggest that you get yourself and your family well protected.'

Broker nods in Lauren and Anne's direction. 'This is why Zeb's got Bear and Chloe hovering around Cassandra,' he adds as they file out of Connor's apartment.

Once outside Connor's apartment, Zeb turns to Bear and Chloe and asks them to be even more vigilant with Cassandra. 'I'm not convinced Connor will leave this alone, and if he includes Holt in his story, then that crazy might do anything.'

Turning to Broker, he adds, 'It might be good if you kept your distance and got back to your information business. You've neglected it long enough.'

Broker gives him the finger. 'I'm sticking closer to you than a wart on your ass. Focus on how we deal with Holt now. I don't think the FBI are going to release Holt, so how long are you going to play nice?'

'I'm going to the DRC's mission at the UN and tell them everything. I expect them to burn the wires to Washington or wherever and lodge this issue with the Secretary-General.'

'Well, hell, why didn't you do this before?'

Zeb shrugs. 'Time was on our side. Now it isn't.'

'I think I'll tag along. You have a habit of finding trouble... even your shadow steers clear of you.'

'Don't. I'll go alone. You try to find out where Holt is holed up. Do another search, this time for houses or apartments that have been leased out in the last two to three months to start with.'

'I end up doing the dirty work while you get the glory,' grumbles Broker as they part.

The next day sees Zeb struggling to get around the Congo's bureaucratic reception desk to set up a meeting at their mission in the UN. Exasperated, he puts his phone down, thinks for a moment, and then dials a number he thought he would never have to use.

'Hello,' says the dry precise voice.

'Sir, this is Zeb, Zebadiah Carter. We met–'

'I remember, Major. How can I help you? I didn't think I would hear from you again,' says the Secretary-General.

Zeb explains his predicament to him and goes silent as the Secretary-General thinks.

'Major, may I ask why you want to meet with them?'

'I would rather you didn't, sir.'

'Is this related to Luvungi?' and then he continues when Zeb doesn't reply, 'Of course – it has to be. Very well. Someone will be in touch with you.'

A couple of days later, Zeb gets the call from the DRC mission asking him to meet with the Permanent Representative of the DRC in the UN.

Jimmy Atoki, a tall African with regal bearing, is waiting for Zeb once he has cleared security. After introductions, he leads the way silently to his offices, and once there, he regards Zeb, expressionless.

'Major, I have taken time to meet you because I got an intriguing call from the Secretary-General suggesting that meeting you would be worthwhile to my country.' He gestures to Zeb, saying, 'Make it worth my while.'

Zeb looks around, taking his time to frame his words,

knowing that the PR's office would be recording the conversation.

The PR observes him with a knowing look. 'You requested this meeting, Major. It's a bit late to be thinking about blowback.'

Zeb looks back at him and does something he has never done in a long time: takes a leap of faith. He tells him everything, without naming the agency or the key players in it.

The PR sits without moving, without emotion, looking right into Zeb's eyes as he listens.

'An interesting story, Major. Luvungi happened, but why should I believe it happened the way you say it did? Back home the story is that it was a bunch of rebel soldiers who committed the atrocities.'

'Sir, there is no reason for me to spin a story and waste your time and mine. I have been to your country a few times. There are a few people in your current government who can vouch for me.'

Atoki's eyebrows rise as Zeb mentions a name. He gestures towards a telephone and lifts it when Zeb gestures a 'sure' back.

Atoki speaks in rapid-fire French to the person at the other end, raises his eyebrows, then hangs up the phone.

'You are well connected, Major,' he says in French, the official language of the Congo.

'Requirements of the job,' Zeb replies in the same language, impressing the PR twice in as many minutes.

'So you want us to shake your FBI tree and be a nuisance so that you can deal with this Holt? And what will you do with Holt once you capture him?'

'That will depend, sir, upon how we capture him.'

A silence fills the room, and then Atoki smiles faintly. 'And if you arrest him as he is jaywalking?'

'I shall hand him over to you.'

The smile grows brighter and then fades as Atoki stares into the distance, letting the silence build, noting that Zeb is relaxed, yet alert. 'Very well. We'll see what falls out when we shake that tree. No doubt you'll discover how successful we are through your connections.'

He escorts Zeb out, and as Zeb is leaving, he calls out, 'Major.'

Zeb turns back.

'We are a nation rich in minerals and yet a poor nation. Our people fight one another and others while our women and children die of hunger. Many here' – he indicates the UN – 'look down on us and deem us unworthy of their attention. But we are also a proud nation. We would not want to see Holt live a comfortable life.'

Zeb looks at him, tall, dark and hard angles, comfortable in a Western milieu but equally comfortable in the warrior's garb in the plains of Africa.

'You are Zande?' Zeb asks.

Atoki inclines his head.

'Holt will not live.'

Atoki looks at him. Zeb is standing relaxed, something in his eyes that Atoki recognizes, another warrior who would be equally comfortable in the African plains. Atoki nods.

Zeb leaves the building. At the gates he sees Broker waiting in a Jeep.

He *knows* immediately.

Broker speeds off without a word as soon as he seats himself.

'What?'

'Lauren and Rory.'

Chapter 16

Broker looks at Zeb out of the corner of his eye. No reaction, not a single muscle twitch on his face, just a quiet stillness surrounds the most lethal man he has ever come across.

He sends the Jeep barreling through New York, through red lights and pedestrian crossings, controlled madness at the wheel, motion unleashed on the streets. The streetlights whiz past, etching streams of light on Broker's face.

'He made a big mistake,' Zeb says finally, and Broker just nods.

It is time to rectify the mistake.

Bear and Chloe are outside the apartment and nod in greeting. They are alert, and the bulges under their jackets are reassuring.

Inside, Connor is slumped over in his armchair, with Anne and Mark fussing over him when they reach his apartment.

Cassandra briefs them calmly.

Lauren and Rory had gone to play in the park after Rory's return from school, and they never returned. Connor organized a frantic search for them when he came home from work, but he couldn't find any trace of them.

Before he could call the police, he received an anonymous call. The message was chilling.

Lauren and Rory had been abducted, and Connor should stay by his phone for further instructions.

'I should have listened to you.' Connor looks at him with dull eyes. 'I wrote my story the day you told me about Holt and included him in it. I contacted Hardinger, wanting to get a quote from him before running it. He denied knowing Holt, just as you said he would. In fact, he denied everything in the story and said he would sue me into oblivion.

'I then told him that there were eyewitnesses to Holt's atrocities in Africa and the photograph linked him directly to Holt. My ego got the better of me, and I mentioned you by name.

'I returned home and...' He trails off, waving his hand around helplessly.

'What did the caller tell you?' Broker asks.

'That I should stay by the phone and not call the police. That I should await instructions.'

Broker turns to Zeb. 'He's moved fast in just one day.

Assuming it's Holt.'

'It's Holt. He said he was Holt,' says Connor.

Zeb nods and looks at Broker. 'Can you–'

'Of course I can. I have everything in the Jeep.' Broker cuts him off and heads out.

'Shouldn't we be calling the police, the FBI?' Anne asks.

Zeb looks at Connor. 'Yes.'

Zeb drifts outside and joins Broker in his Jeep.

Broker is looking at some graphical image on his laptop. 'I narrowed down the recently leased houses in Williamstown to about ten, and I'm looking into who rented them.'

'If a phone got turned on in any of those houses, would you be able to pinpoint which house it was?'

Broker looks up and catches on where Zeb is going with this. 'Do fish fuck in the ocean?' He narrows his eyes. 'What are you doing out here? Shouldn't you be creating an action plan with Connor? And why are we doing this shit, anyway? The NYPD or the FBI can hunt Holt down and rescue them. This has gone way beyond WITSEC now. The FBI can't stand by their witness protection story anymore.

'Oh, all right,' he growls when Zeb continues to stare at him, and gets back to his laptop. 'I'm into the systems of the different cell phone networks and am using a better system than the FBI or the NYPD use to triangulate. If a call originated from those houses, we'll know which house it came from.'

He looks up when a sedan approaches them and parks in front just a few feet away from the nose of their Jeep. Isakson gets out and strides inside without noticing them, followed by a couple of agents.

'The cavalry to the rescue. Now the world will be saved,' Broker sneers. 'I bet he asks us to disappear.'

'They'll come to us.' Zeb reclines in his seat and closes his eyes.

'Did a little angel whisper that in your ear? You know that how?'

'Figure it out for yourself.'

An hour later they're back in the apartment after one of Isakson's agents summoned them.

'Like we're his flunkies,' grumbles Broker.

'How can we help you, sir?' he asks Isakson politely.

'Our profilers have been working on Holt, and they think he'll want to talk to you or meet you.'

'No shit. That must have been a very hard deduction given that Zeb has been hounding him for ages and Mr. Balthazar went ahead and mentioned Zeb to Holt.'

Isakson's face darkens, but he controls himself. 'Will you take his call if he asks for you?'

'Yes,' replies Zeb for the first time. 'How did all this happen?'

Isakson looks away. 'We don't know. He came in every day to our offices and was giving us good intel. A couple of days ago, he stopped coming. We tried calling him but got no response. We suspect he found out about Mr. Balthazar here and his story through the Senator and cut loose. The Senator has been called in for questioning.'

'Your story's got him.' Broker nods in Connor's direction.

Connor laughs mirthlessly. 'The script didn't read like this.'

'Why didn't you surround Holt's freaking place, tear it down, and bust his ass?' Broker growls at Isakson.

'We didn't have his address,' Isakson admits, clearly embarrassed, but also angry.

He sees Broker's disbelief and continues, 'We tried tracking him down, but he always ended up giving us the slip. We tried slipping monitoring devices on him, but he detected those and threw them away. As you know, one of the conditions of his intel was that he'd get witness protection, but we never reached that stage. We thought he was holding back on some vital intel, and hence, we were going slowly on WITSEC.'

A long silence fills the room.

'Bastards. Surely you lowlifes were not too dumb to see that this was a car crash waiting to happen. That Holt would do anything to either get away from Zeb or go after him?' Broker throws up his hands.

A muscle in Isakson's face begins to tic. 'This is not the time for recriminations. We should focus on negotiating with Holt and securing the safe release of Lauren and Rory. I'm expecting our profiling and negotiating team shortly to help us on this. All I'm asking is for you to take the call if he asks for you. Save the superstar act for another day.'

Zeb doesn't move, doesn't say anything, his presence filling the room, and turns and walks out silently.

'That's his way of saying he'll take the call.' Broker looks at Isakson, the 'asshole' at the end left unsaid but understood by all.

Zeb returns once the profilers and negotiators arrive.

'How will you do this? Who will talk to him when he calls?' Cassandra asks.

'Mr. Balthazar will speak to him first. The negotiators are here to help him. If he asks for Major Carter, then he is here to take that call. There are no rules for this. Each hostage situation is driven by the circumstances, and we adapt and take control as we go along.'

Broker has set up his hardware and is going through all his feeds. One of the agents whistles when he sees Broker's equipment.

'Private enterprise and no red tape,' Broker says, with a wink.

When the call comes, Zeb recognizes the emotionless voice immediately from agency tapes.

'Mr. Balthazar, I have your wife and son here with me. You know what I want: all your photographs, your notes, your emails, and anything you've written on this subject so far. The original ones, please. In return you get your wife and son back...intact.'

One of the negotiating team gestures to Connor, and he asks, 'How do I know they're even alive?'

'Mr. Balthazar, what good would they be to me dead? Wouldn't I lose my negotiating strength? I'm guessing that you're surrounded by the FBI, who are guiding you, and you have profilers looking over your shoulder reading into every voice inflection of mine.

'Is my friend Isakson there? Hello, Isak? I know you're there, and I know you were stringing me along. But guess what, asshole? I was stringing you along, too. Most of the shit I gave you was so old and useless that it had even stopped stinking. But I guess you guys are so desperate to find the Ts under any and every rock that you'll bend over and spread 'em for anyone who sings about them.'

Isakson's face becomes thunderous, and his agents shift uneasily, but he keeps quiet.

Broker is studying his laptop, trying to locate where the signal is coming from.

Holt's voice hardens. 'Oh, and, Mr. Balthazar, who does the exchange is important. If you want to see your wife and son again, then Carter is the one I want to bring all your shit to me. I'm betting he's there right now. Why don't you put him on?'

Connor looks up helplessly at Zeb, who steps forward and takes the phone.

'Holt?'

'Ah, Major. We meet again, if this can be called a meeting.'

'The first time was also not a meeting. You turned tail while I was dispatching your friends.'

Holt pauses. 'The past. Let's plan the exchange. Tomorrow afternoon at Grand Central. You alone, with my criminal record in a manila envelope.' He chuckles. 'And you can take the lovely Mrs. Balthazar and the brat back.'

'Penn Station. The exchange will be at Penn,' Zeb counters.

Holt laughs incredulously. 'Back up, Major. Read the script. I'm the one with the hostages. You do as I say.'

Zeb hangs up. He looks at Broker, who mouths silently, 'Some more time.'

Isakson strides to Zeb and shoves him away from the phone.

A blur of motion too fast for Connor to register and Isakson is lying on his back with Zeb's foot on his throat.

Bear and Broker have cornered Isakson's agents.

After a tense second, Zeb takes his foot off Isakson and pulls him up. He turns his back on the FBI agent, allowing him to gather himself, his dignity, and lower the tension in the room.

When Zeb turns back to them, he behaves as if he hadn't dumped Isakson on his ass, and they all take that cue.

Broker goes back to his laptop, and Bear leaves the room.

Connor swallows his shock and asks Zeb, 'Why did you hang up? Aren't you risking my family by this? Wouldn't it have been better to continue talking so that the FBI could trace his call?'

'He'll call back.'

'Like fuck he will,' replies Isakson angrily.

'Boss, he did the right thing, not giving Holt control,' pipes up a diffident voice, one of the profilers.

Isakson whirls on him just as Broker murmurs, 'And these guys are supposed to protect us?'

'I heard that,' Isakson shouts, 'and anyway, what are you doing in that corner?'

The phone rings. 'Don't fucking hang up on me, you bastard! Who the fuck do you think you are?' Holt shouts.

Zeb hangs up again.

The third call comes less than a minute later.

'You want to see these two dead? You know what I'm capable of!'

'I am least interested in the two of them. I'm here just because you asked for me and I know Mr. Balthazar. As far as I'm concerned, you're a dead man walking. You have run out of fuel and are running on fumes.'

He hangs up again, and out of the corner of his eye, he can see Broker nodding.

Isakson is peering over the shoulders of his tech guys to see if they've triangulated the call. From his expression he can see that the agents aren't having much luck. Broker, on the other hand, uses tech that's a few years ahead of the FBI or the NSA or any other agency. Broker buys start-ups that specialize in security and surveillance, takes them off the market and then uses them in his business.

The phone rings again.

'You had better not ring again if you have any stupid demands to make,' Zeb tells him and looks across at Connor, who is drawing in a shocked breath.

There is silence from Holt then. 'What do you want?'

'The exchange will be tomorrow evening at Penn Station.' Zeb names the exact location and hangs up.

Isakson replies to Connor's unasked question of *what now?* 'The Major here will go make the exchange alone, but not really. We'll surround the place with undercover agents and rescue your wife and son. I'm surprised that Holt agreed to this so readily, though.'

Broker snorts. 'He won't be there. If I were him, once I calmed down, I'd realize that I still hold all the cards. I'd go to the exchange, hide, and observe Zeb and whoever else comes with him. I'd then call him and arrange an exchange at another place. Zeb would have no choice but to comply.'

Turning to Connor, he adds, 'With respect, sir, I don't want you to have false hopes. This man is dangerous, and unfortunately for us, he's smart, too. The fact that he's walking around free after mass murder proves how smart he is. He has the FBI by the balls because they were harboring and sheltering him, and that's something they will desperately not want to go public. Your family will be back, but it may not be tomorrow.'

That muscle in Isakson's cheek twitches again, but he refrains from striking back. He nods reluctantly in Connor's direction. 'He may be right. All I can say is we will do everything possible to get your family back.'

Broker pushes his chair back and puts his equipment away as Zeb gets up and tells Connor, 'Your family will be back – safe.' Then he nods at Isakson. 'See you tomorrow to work out the logistics.'

Bear and Chloe slip out as they leave. 'What was that with the hang-ups? Weren't you taking a risk?'

'Yup,' Broker replies, 'but we wanted to able to pinpoint where the phone signal was coming from and needed a few cut-outs to be sure.'

He goes on to explain how they knew what to look for. 'A couple of years back, I came across a couple of Chinese students at Stanford who had developed a triangulating software program. A mobile phone's location can be detected within a tower's grid by the signal it gives out. The FBI, NSA, CIA...all those guys use this to locate a phone – but it gives you a very rough location. These Chinese guys went one step ahead. They mapped this triangulation against two other signals, one – the radiation signal of the phone, the other – something called location leaks. A mobile phone service provider keeps a database of where phones are likely to be and keeps polling the phones so that it's quicker to connect when a call happens. These polling messages were used by these two guys as the third triangulator. I bought their software before they went to market. But it does require a few cut-outs to home in on the phone.'

Bear nods. 'So what's the plan now?'

'We come back tomorrow, take orders from the big cheese.'

Bear smiles at Zeb and Broker and then gets serious. 'You're going in tonight?'

'Yep.'

'I'll tag along.'

'Nope. I need you here.'

Bear nods, grips Zeb's shoulder hard, fist-bumps Broker, and goes back inside the apartment.

Broker looks at Zeb. 'How about a fancy, motivating speech?'

Zeb grunts and moves past him.

'That'll do,' says Broker. 'For a moment I thought you

would bring me to tears. Where to now?'

'Weapons, wheels, Williamstown. That's where he is, isn't he? His mother's house?'

'Right. Anyone ever tell you, you talk a lot? And what's wrong with these wheels?' He indicates the shiny red Jeep they have driven in.

Zeb says nothing, just taps the red paint.

'Okay.' He buckles up and turns to Zeb. 'What do you think Isakson will say when he hears about this?'

Zeb stares straight ahead. 'What do you think we'll say to ourselves if that kid doesn't return tomorrow?'

He revs the engine in the ensuing silence.

The first few stops are at the various caches he has in the city, and they load up with night vision, Mossberg shotguns, the AWM rifle, an Armalite, Sig Sauers, and Glocks.

'You know that's a residential neighborhood?' Broker reminds him.

He answers himself when Zeb doesn't respond. 'The residents should have known better, obviously.'

They pack the equipment, then switch their vehicle to a Hummer Broker has customized. Zeb scans the interior, noticing the mobile and wireless communication system, radar and various switches and gadgets that would make James Bond envious.

He casually flicks one, and out pops a screen that shows a rocket launcher easing out of its recess beneath the chassis. He flicks an eyebrow at Broker, who waves his arms in the direction of downtown Manhattan.

'The neighborhood. It's not what it used to be.'

Broker turns serious, pulls out a map of Williamstown, and lays it out on the hood. He traces a finger around Mama Holt's property. 'Close to the street, six bedrooms, three stories, large windows both at the front and back, tall hedge surrounding the gardens, neighboring houses not too far off, neighbors might remember you from earlier visits...not easy, but would we enjoy it if it was easy?' He looks sideways at Zeb, who listens calmly.

'How many men would you have about you, in his situation?' he asks Zeb.

'Six or seven in the house including myself.'

Broker nods. 'Was thinking the same. How do you want to do it?' He rolls out the house plan and lays it next to the street plan.

Zeb examines the house plan for a long time. 'Flat or sloping roof?' he asks, already knowing the answer.

'Sloping.'

'I need some special equipment.'

'I can get you anything, even a frigging aircraft carrier, in one hour within ten clicks.'

He folds the maps and puts them away when Zeb nods, and throws the keys to him. 'Drive.' And Zeb does, leaving New York behind.

They reach Williamstown at dusk, with Zeb making one pass of the street and parking in a faraway parking lot. Hoofing it back, they flit from shadow to shadow, observing the entire street, the foliage, its dark spots, the streetlights and proximity of the houses.

They hide in thick foliage by the side of the street a house away. They have a good view of Holt's house, which has a well-lit front, darkened windows and just a smidgen of light in the window of the second floor.

'Watch out for dogs,' mutters Broker.

Broker takes out a pair of night-vision goggles, parabolic mics and a thermal-imaging monitor, setting the screen with a filter that protects it from detection even from six inches away.

Both of them don the mics and watch the house and imager alternatively.

'Two bodies downstairs, four in the middle, and two more upstairs; lot of light in the front. They can be in the dark of the house, spot us, and pick us off without a problem,' murmurs Broker as the blobs appear on the monitor. The blobs at the top and bottom of the house are moving back and forth at regular intervals.

'Sentries covering the front and back of the house. No windows to the side of the house,' whispers Broker.

They settle down and try to pick up any noise, but either the mics are not powerful enough or the house is well insulated, and they hear nothing. In the middle floor only one blob is pacing; the others are stationary, with two blobs next to one another. Broker taps the two blobs, pulls up his watch, and starts to time the sentries.

'They alternate from back to front every ten minutes. Pause in front of each window, look around, and then walk back.

No head popping out of a window, which is good for us, bad for them. As usual, good help is always hard to come by. One sentry either at the top or bottom is always covering the two sides. We need final confirmation, and I don't see how we're going to get that unless we can hear or see them.'

Broker looks at him sideways. 'Uh-oh, don't even think of going in the garden on a recon round. Suicide missions are so last week. They could be looking out the windows, and pop goes the weasel!'

Zeb opens Broker's backpack, removes an earbud and collar mic, and puts them on. He hands another pair to Broker, who gives a long-suffering sigh and does the same.

'Where?' he asks Broker.

Broker shakes his head. 'Cross Keys, not far from here. Driving directions are keyed in.' He waves in the direction of the Hummer.

Zeb takes the keys and sets off, pointing in the direction of his earbud and collar mic in response to Broker's urgent, 'How will I know when you're back?'

Broker settles into the darkness, takes out a range finder from his kit, and checks out the range to Holt's house even though he has gauged the distance down to the last inch. He assembles the AWM, sights, zeros it, and lays it down again.

He then calls Bear and briefs him on the situation and in return hears an earful of curses. 'Hold your horses. I did tell him, but you know him. Once he has a plan in mind, only changed circumstances deter him. No, you stay there.'

* * *

Zeb reaches Cross Keys airport and finds a Super Otter waiting for him, with its pilot leaning against the fuselage.

'You Zeb Carter?'

Zeb nods.

'Broker told me about what you want done. Have you done this before? It's foolhardy to–'

Zeb waves him off, signs the disclaimer papers, and checks out the kit that the pilot has brought for him.

'Dude, you do know what you're doing, don't you?' the pilot asks, conscious of lawsuits.

Zeb ignores him and unfolds the kit and lays it on the tarmac. He inspects it fully and then folds it carefully and takes it inside the plane. The pilot has unfolded an aerial map of Williamstown and is tracing their route when Zeb rejoins him.

'This is where I want to be,' Zeb tells him, pointing to the exact location.

The pilot does his calculations. 'You're lucky it's not very windy, but it *is* dark.'

'Dark is good. Let's go.'

The Super Otter roars to life in the stillness of the night and takes off after a short taxiing run. The pilot swings wide away from Williamstown and climbs to 13,000 feet and then takes a long circle back to Williamstown.

The pilot looks over his shoulder when he's twenty miles away from Williamstown.

He sees Batman.

Zeb and Broker had discussed the best way to approach and enter Holt's house and had eventually agreed, though Broker would vehemently deny it, on a wing-suit jump. The unknowns were too many to risk any other kind of approach. Holt was likely to have access to sophisticated surveillance, and the closeness of the neighborhood made even a covert approach risky. The one factor that finally got Broker to agree to what he thought was a suicidal approach was Holt's personality. They just didn't know enough about Holt to risk being detected in any other approach. For all they knew, Holt would kill Lauren and Rory and go down shooting, since he'd no longer have anything to lose.

Zeb has strapped up the US Special Forces wing suit that Broker has mysteriously procured and puts on the backpack that contains the square canopy parachute, reserve chute, and oxygen bottles, and adjusts the shoulder and leg straps. He then dons the helmet, adjusts the oxygen mask receivers, and after checking the suit instruments, asks the pilot the wind velocity and direction. The pilot shouts back at him and then warns him they are fifteen miles away from Williamstown.

Zeb pushes open the door of the aircraft, causing the aircraft to judder before the pilot brings it under control, steadies himself on the frame, and waits for the pilot's signal.

The pilot steadies the aircraft, and when they hit a patch of clear sky, he lifts his thumb to Zeb.

Zeb dives into the dark and spreads the suit wide open to steady himself once clear of the plane.

In the distance he sees the taillights of the aircraft disappearing, and below, vast emptiness. The suit has a glide ratio of 3:1 and is fully equipped with a navigation system, altimeter and various gadgets to help the flight. Zeb has already fallen a thousand feet since his jump and is eleven miles from Williamstown.

At a hundred and twenty-five miles per hour, with the wind rushing in his face, darkness around him, he is alone in the universe, but then, Zeb has been alone all his life.

He plans his landing and every step he will take once he lands. After a few minutes he can see lights far below and, ahead of him, pinpricks piercing the dark, playing hide and seek with the clouds.

He steers in their direction, guided by the navigation system, and sets himself up a glide path. There is a mild headwind slowing his descent, but it will help him once he opens his chute. He makes a mental check of the weapons and kit he is carrying. Given the wing-suit approach, he has had to be very selective in what he can carry, just a couple of handguns, a knife, his cable camera, and night-vision goggles.

His suit starts beeping when he's four thousand feet away, indicating that he is nearing the chute-opening altitude. He opens his chute at three thousand five hundred and feels the kick on his back and the slowing down of his speed as it unfolds without any hitches. He can see it above his head, a dark shadow in the surrounding darkness. Below, Williamstown is growing with every second, the lights and the town becoming clearer with every foot he falls.

He enlarges the map on the navigation system and starts toggling the chute across to move above Holt's house. There's a slight headwind he has to compensate for, and he descends vertically. From his surveillance and topography, he knows that the roof of Holt's house isn't surrounded by trees, so all he has to do is land soundlessly on a sloping roof. He can imagine Broker snorting at that – he has had far more difficult landings than this on other missions.

He clears his mind and focuses on the fast-approaching terrain below, now sharp and clear; the street lighting casting a yellow glow, a flame Zeb is rushing toward.

Zeb toggles the chute gently until he's dropping slowly over the roof of Holt's house, bends his knees, pulls both brakes, and steps out of the sky onto the house, balancing himself on the incline of the roof. He quickly unstraps the chute, pulls it down, and crumples it to its smallest. The wing suit joins the chute as he steps out of it, dressed now in his hunting gear, all black with his guns and knife strapped across his body. From his backpack he takes a long cord that he wraps around the wing suit and chute, and ties both to the chimney so that they don't flap in the night or fall down to the ground and draw attention from within.

He double-clicks his collar mic, waits for Broker to respond and, when he does, double-clicks again to signal over and out.

He wraps another rope around the chimney of the house, wraps the other end of it around his waist, and lowers himself down the front of the house between the windows. He lowers himself down a foot and stops immediately. In all their planning, Broker and he had overlooked a simple and now glaring fact – the house clapboards are painted white, and Zeb is in black.

He wills away his anger at his mistake, knowing that Broker is watching and has caught on to the challenge. He waits a few minutes, working out various options, and then decides to take the risk and continue. The traffic is almost nonexistent, and neighboring houses are dark.

The front has six large windows, but Zeb is interested in only one – the one on the second floor that had the three blobs in it. Back in New York, Broker and he had worked out the angle at which he would have to lower himself so that the only way anyone from any window would spot him would be if they leaned far out of the window. So far none of the sentries seem to be so inclined.

He hopes his luck holds out.

He lowers himself to a few feet from the top of the window and then pulls out a telescopic wire camera. He has his Glock strapped to his left arm in case somebody decides to get a breath of night air. Broker modified the wire camera – it's fitted with night-vision capabilities that can be turned on and off, and also a wireless capability with a limited range.

Zeb activates the wireless unit and hears an acknowledging double-click from Broker as the images come up on Broker's monitor. He lowers the camera to the top corner of the window and positions it and finds the curtain obstructing the view. He moves the camera towards the central divide in the curtain, finds no luck there either, and moves the camera down the divide. At a narrow opening at the bottom, he gets lucky and is able to see inside, but all he sees are legs – three pairs of them sitting, two pairs facing the third – and a dim light burning in the room. The camera is on a downward angle, and he is unable to correct the angle to make it horizontal, so he moves it to the top right corner of the window. He gets lucky there and gets a clear view of Holt, with Lauren and Rory, both gagged, facing him, their profiles to the window.

Broker double-clicks, acknowledging the images on his screen.

Holt is looking straight at the camera as if he knows it's there. Zeb keeps it still, hoping it's too small to be detected by Holt – especially in the dark.

After his contemplation, Holt looks away and says something to Lauren, who nods. Zeb commits everything in the room to memory, where Lauren and Rory are seated, Holt's chair – whatever the camera sees, Zeb absorbs.

He considers peering through the other windows but drops the idea immediately when he studies them. They are all dark from within and without curtains; he or his camera would be easily spotted.

He climbs back up the wall and steadies himself on the roof as he gets rid of the climbing rope, planning his entry all the while. There should be a skylight on the side of the roof facing the back.

This is his point of entry.

He moves cautiously up the peak of the roof and surveys the other side.

No skylight.

Chapter 17

He can't tear his eyes away from the smooth downward slope of the roof. He looks away for a moment and then turns back to the roof.

Nope. His eyes aren't playing tricks. There isn't a skylight.

The wing suit approach was because of the existence of a skylight, which was marked on the house plan Broker found.

Clearly Holt had rebuilt the roof to eliminate that entry point. He must have considered filling in the windows, but that would have drawn attention to the house. Zeb leans against the chimney and considers his options. It's obvious he'll have to go in through a window – the middle window on the top floor, facing the rear, winning hands down against the other windows.

Zeb signals Broker with a small flashlight to get his attention.

Broker replies with a text message, and when Zeb answers it, back comes a string of curses. 'I knew there would be a fuckup. It was too easy till now.' Another string of curses follow and then a few minutes of silence.

'Top floor has two men patrolling the front and back windows on either side of the house. These same two guys alternately patrol the middle windows too. Each man spends about ten minutes in the rear room where the middle window at the back is located. The room is without a patrol every ten minutes, so that's your opportunity. You'll have to use that.

'Keep your phone powered on. I'll message when the window is clear at the next ten-minute interval.'

'No need. Will figure out. No more now,' Zeb replies and powers off his mobile, removes the battery, and pockets both.

He peers down the back of the house and works out an approach to the middle window, wraps the rope around his waist, and sets down noiselessly to just above the sill of the window. He extends the wire camera and plugs it into the top left corner of the window, a corner that is usually overlooked by right-handed men, the most common handedness on the planet.

The room is dark, but the images stand out clearly, courtesy of the improvements Broker has made to the camera. He can make out furniture – a wardrobe, a bed against the wall – and in the distance the faint glow of the open door.

He waits, something he is very good at.

The guard drifts in eight minutes later and positions himself by the side of the door and stands still.

A good move, thinks Zeb, *a sign of experience.* An inexperienced guard would move to the window immediately. The guard drifts to the sides of the room and then approaches the window but stands a few feet and to the side, observing the world outside. All good tradecraft except for not checking outside the windows.

Zeb waits till the guard leaves and then slithers down rapidly to the side of the window. Bracing his legs against the wall, he withdraws a suction cup from his backpack, attaches it just above the sash, and cuts a circle around it with a diamond cutter. He removes the circle of glass and drops it behind his head into the open mouth of his backpack.

Most houses of that age have windows with locking mechanisms at the bottom, and luckily these windows have a simple sliding bolt screwed into the frame. It takes Zeb not more than a couple of minutes to unscrew the bolt, open the window, and slip inside.

He glances at his watch – six minutes from first tapping on the window. He can imagine Broker snorting in disgust, for Zeb has made similar entries in less than five minutes with hurricane winds eddying around him.

He mentally shrugs, moves to the far wall, and stands with his back to it a few feet away from the door. He rests lightly on his feet, becoming one with the house, his mind entering a grey zone where only motion and silence exist.

One of the sentries would be back in about four minutes by his reckoning, and a stealthy footfall outside the room signals his arrival. Lithe and wiry, the man entering the room is not Jones, the last surviving member of the Rogue Six, barring Holt himself. He enters the room slowly and immediately spots the open window and the circle cut in it. He steps forward and then turns back swiftly, spinning on his right foot, his right arm coming up with the Sig Sauer he had been holding at his side.

Zeb anticipates that move, coming under his arm and squeezing his wrist in a bone crusher with his left arm, and renders him unconscious with two blows to a nerve center at the side of his neck. He then twists his neck sharply to break it. He searches the body, which is in its death throes.

No communication equipment, not even a wallet. Maybe Holt and the guards communicate by calling out.

He drags the body to the far corner of the room and covers it with a dark bedspread.

Zeb pauses just inside the door to listen for the other guard at the opposite end of the house.

Nothing.

Outside the room is a broad corridor running the breadth of the house, with two rooms on either side at either end of the corridor, and a large bathroom in between, opposite the room Zeb's in. Opposite the bathroom and slightly off it is the staircase that goes to the lower floors. Zeb lies down on the floor and cautiously peers out the door and down the passage. He can see the rooms at the far ends and the door to the bathroom, but no other guard.

He slips across the passage, checks the rooms closest to him, finds them empty, as he expected, then goes to the front windows to peer across the garden and the street. All he can see is the street and a dark shadow behind it, the hedge line. He's not sure if Broker can spot him.

It doesn't matter.

He goes back to the door, listens, and then glances out.

No one.

He glides across to the bathroom, large and luxurious, with a Jacuzzi for four, which Broker would have commented on, makes sure it's unoccupied, and then returns to the door.

Three long strides will take him past the staircase and to the doors of the last two rooms at the other end of the house, where the other sentry should be. He takes four, walking purposefully but not hurrying.

His luck runs out when he crosses the stairs.

The other guard steps out of the far room at the back and looks to the left, straight at Zeb. Zeb is a dark shadow amidst the dark of the house, and the guard looks back to the room ahead after his casual glance to the left. He takes a half step forward, does a double take, and spins back toward Zeb, his mouth opening in a shout, his hand lifting his gun.

In Zeb's world, reaction times are in milliseconds, and this guard is fast.

Incredibly fast.

In Zeb's world, incredibly fast means incredibly dead.

Zeb blurred into motion even as the gunman was turning

around. His shoulder slams into the guard, knocking the wind out of him and deterring his alarm call to the rest of the pack. Zeb takes a step to the side, grabs the guard's hair, and cuts his throat. The throat has strong muscles and tissue, and usually a sawing motion is what it really takes to cut a throat. Not now, not here. Zeb is all motion and fire, currents of energy surging through his body, centering on the blade of his knife, which goes in cleanly. The gunman's body fountains his blood out in large spurts.

Zeb lays the body down and searches it.

This gunman isn't carrying a mic or headset either.

He's alert for any approaching sounds from the floor below but doesn't detect any. The floors are thick and solid, and that's probably deadened the scuffle.

Two down, four to go.

The plan, Broker had looked bemused at that description, called for Zeb to take out the gunmen on the top floor and then go to the hostage room to neutralize Holt. Broker would take out the other gunmen on the ground floor with his long gun as soon as Zeb entered the hostage room. The last gunman on the second floor, other than Holt, would be dealt with by Zeb or Broker as the situation presented itself.

The stairs to the second floor are wooden and thickly carpeted, with a landing between the floors.

He hugs the wall and tests the first step.

No creak.

He moves down cautiously and checks around the landing. The second floor is brightly lit but, from what he can see of it, empty.

Once he reaches the bottom of the stairs, on his right will be the hostage room, on his left the rooms the third gunman is patrolling, and in front, a bathroom.

Zeb goes down the last flight casually yet alert and slips into the bathroom opposite, his knife ready.

It's empty.

Out of the corner of his eye, while crossing the passage, he sees someone with his back to him in the room to his right, the hostage room.

Getting to his knees, he uncoils his wire camera and places it under the door. Swiveling the lens toward the rooms with the patrol, he times the appearance of the guard.

The guard appears a few minutes later, going from the

rear room to the front, and returns after ten minutes. The resolution of the image is too small for Zeb to make out if it's Jones, but he doesn't think so. Too short.

He turns the camera toward the hostage room and makes out the edges of a couple of chairs, but not much else. There is a faint murmur coming from that room. He waits for the guard at the other end to repeat his ten-minute routine, and when he disappears into the rear room, Zeb walks out.

He has left his backpack and his entire kit, other than his Glock, a couple of clips and his knife, in the bathroom.

He hugs the left wall so that he can get the widest angle into the hostage room, and just as he nears the door, he sees them.

Lauren and Rory are bound and gagged in two chairs facing the door at an angle. The room, what he can see of it, has a dining table and a few chairs, a bookshelf on one wall, but not much else by way of furniture. All this in a glance as he tries to locate Holt.

He pauses just outside the door, trying to figure out what Lauren and Rory, who have spotted him, are trying to signal with their eyes. They tensed up initially when they saw him and then consciously relaxed, but their eyes are giving him mixed signals.

He moves in, spots Holt, his back to the door. He's staring out of the window.

Conscious that the guard behind him might reappear in the passage at any minute, Zeb steps into the room, moves silently to the right, close to the wall, closer to Holt. His pulse slows, stillness flowing through him.

Holt senses something, stiffens and, without looking back, says, 'So here you are, Major Carter. I've been expecting you. Clearly my guys upstairs weren't as good as I thought.'

'Turn around slowly.'

He hears a window shatter and knows what that means. Broker protecting his back.

Holt laughs. 'Is that what I think it is? Damn, your timing's bad. I was planning to have some fun with the Balthazar bitch. You know, I've fucked so many niggers in Luvungi that I've forgotten what it is to have some white pussy.'

Lauren is chalk white and trembling violently.

Rory has gone into shock and isn't reacting to much.

Zeb is breathing slowly and easily, his heart rate low. He

knows what Holt's doing and what's coming. He has been in these situations a million times, seen many Holts.

And then a door behind the dining table opens.

Chapter 18

The Sig Sauer P229 DAK rises quickly to the gunman's shoulder as he takes a long step in the room. At the same time, Holt is pivoting about smoothly, his right hand holding another Sig Sauer. The new gunman has to compensate for Zeb's position, and his initial burst goes wild, over Zeb's head.

Zeb crouches, his Glock an extension of his arm, the barrel seeing what his eye sees. His first shot drills the gunman's left shoulder, his second shot takes out his forehead, his third burns Holt's right shoulder, who has stepped to his left in anticipation of Zeb's firing.

The furrow makes Holt drop his gun, but his left hand flashes to his back and sends a foot-long knife scything through the air at Zeb.

Holt's knife buries deep in his right shoulder, making him lose his Glock, which bounces away a few feet beyond reach. He has no time to retrieve it as Holt follows up by rushing at him with another blade at the ready.

The time for active thought is gone, animal instinct doing what it does best. It shuts down his conscious thought, freezes his pain, and lets combat training take over.

Zeb dislodges the knife with his left hand and parries Holt's thrust, moving to the center of the room to create more space. A feint by Holt is followed by a quick thrust to Zeb's upper body, the knife low and wicked, and Zeb just slides back and then forward in a return thrust, scratching Holt's wrist on the return. Holt takes a long step back, grabs a dining chair from behind him with one hand, and throws it across at Zeb. He follows the throw with a sinuous charge.

Zeb ducks easily under the chair and, just before Holt reaches him, bends to his left knee, his right leg spinning straight and around, knocking Holt's right knee out of its socket. Holt falls heavily to his left, yet rolls back, grabs another chair by its leg, and heaves it over his shoulder at Zeb.

A wild throw that misses Zeb by a good foot and a half.

Just as he's bending down, he senses danger behind him, and he ducks and takes a long step to the side, but his bending and twisting is arrested as an arm encircles his neck, choking him. He tries to break the choke hold, letting his knife drop, when he feels a blade pierce him from the left, between his ribs, going deep inside and upwards.

It's a knife probing for his heart. Another gunman who has come up from behind him, who escaped Broker's long gun somehow.

His brain kicks into high alert and starts shutting down nonessential functions in his body.

Dimly Zeb hears the sound of Holt laughing as he lies a few feet away, and that drives him to a deep, raw rage. He forces himself to go into his grey zone where the impossible happens, grabs hold of his rage, shapes it into a raw ball of fire growing tighter and harder and hotter, and then shapes that fire into a spear flowing from inside him to his arms. Instead of moving away from the knife, he pushes back into his assailant, his right hand gripping the wrist wielding the knife, and that spear of energy coils around the wrist, squeezing and squeezing until the bones in the gunman's wrist snap.

The gunman shouts hoarsely in his ear, his knife hand falling away uselessly and his forearm around Zeb's neck loosening.

Zeb twists to his left, falling, the gunman half facing him, his right hand searching and finding and gripping the assailant's throat as he falls and brings the gunman on top of him awkwardly. Zeb squeezes, draining the life out of the gunman, uncaring about the blows against his body, uncaring about the knife sinking deeper into him.

The gunman's thrashings slow down and then stop.

A few feet away, Holt has been watching curiously, and he now rolls over and shoves himself up, dragging his right leg as he approaches Zeb. He picks up Zeb's fallen gun, holding it casually as he stands over Zeb.

'I wonder if you are worth a bullet now, Major. Looks like you will be at the pearly gates soon enough and I'll be gone with these two. The FBI will come after me now, but at least I have the chips on my side and white pussy to keep me company in the dark lonely nights.'

Zeb whispers something.

'Praying, Major? Shall I administer the last rites?' He lifts Zeb's Glock.

The shot is muffled and could be mistaken for a car misfiring distantly. Except that the shot is in the room, and there is no mistaking the red ugly hole in Holt's chest. He looks down stupidly, teetering back on his heels, and Zeb fires again from beneath the gunman's body.

The second blast takes Holt down just as Broker rushes into the room. Taking in Holt and Zeb in one glance, he moves swiftly to cut Lauren and Rory free before kneeling down next to Zeb. He rolls the dead assailant off him and sees the gun in Zeb's right hand, the gun Zeb had taken off the waist of the gunman, sees the knife deep inside him, the blood dripping alongside it.

He grips Zeb's shoulder hard. 'Hold on, buddy. Help's coming. We'll get you back in good enough shape to take a swing at Isakson.'

Zeb looks in his eyes and sees everything there, knows it in his body. He clasps Broker's hand in his own, his breath labored.

The living organism expended all its efforts, all its resources in creating that ball of fire and directing it where needed. Now the need has gone, and the organism is empty, drained by that enormous burst of energy, empty of the survival instinct.

Zeb can feel the stillness flooding him, the room dimming, Rory's face appearing beside Broker's shoulder.

He has no words for Rory.

He closes his eyes, his grip on Broker's hand easing. Darkness floods him, and from far away he sees a pair of bright, mischievous eyes looking at him.

'I'm coming, baby,' he whispers and slips away into the welcoming blackness.

Chapter 19

It's pouring, fierce driving rain battering the windows of New York, the clouds being ripped apart by the occasional streak of lightning.

Connor, looking out the window, adjusting his tie, wonders if the city gets a momentary turn of conscience after such a rain before it lapses into its sell-my-mother-to-get-ahead ways, and then reprimands himself for being silly. After all, he thrives in the razor-sharp living of the city.

Feeling someone behind him, he turns to see Lauren and Rory all dressed up and ready to go. Giving a hug to Rory and a kiss to Lauren, he leads the way to their car.

The two months since Lauren's and Rory's rescue have passed in a blur.

* * *

Isakson, when he learned that fateful night that Zeb had launched his own rescue, had gone incandescent with rage and had vowed to arrest him on sight. He called Broker to find out where Zeb was and where Holt was holed up, but Broker hadn't picked up his phone.

As the night wore on and tempers cooled, Isakson acknowledged that Zeb had the best chance of success, since his team from Quantico wouldn't have reached them in time, and it was likely that Holt would move his base of operations afterward, anyway.

'We are bound by rules, sir, and the Major isn't, but don't ever quote me on that,' he had told him privately much later.

Connor felt only relief, enormous relief, when he heard of the rescue, and had been reduced to helpless tears when the FBI and police had brought his family back to him.

Shame and guilt had set in later when he noticed Cassandra's appearance. Cassandra hadn't uttered a word, had just gone white and swayed a bit and left the apartment, followed by Broker, Bear and Chloe.

Zeb's not surviving the rescue attempt had never occurred to any of them, and it still was hard to grasp two months later. While Connor and his family had known him only for a short while, his dark brooding presence had had a huge impact on them all, especially Rory. Lauren and Rory had gone through several sessions with a shrink, and both seemed to have recovered from their ordeal. Lauren had been a teary-eyed wreck for a few weeks afterward and had turned her gratitude to Zeb into a rage over Connor's job. Time, the shrink, and the solidity of her family around her had helped calm her down and put things into perspective.

The rescue had blown Connor's stories wide open. Hardinger had been arrested, Alchemy was under investigation by numerous federal bodies, and Connor was being feted the length and the breadth of the journalistic world.

The FBI had come under ugly scrutiny but managed to redeem themselves a little by claiming credit for the rescue.

'Assholes.' Broker had shrugged when Connor spoke to him briefly a few days later and didn't say anything more.

Rory had come out of the hostage situation very well, the natural ebullience of youth helping his recovery. Zeb now wasn't just a hero to him but the closest thing to God.

Connor had found out that there had been one other gunman on the second floor that neither Broker nor Zeb had detected with their thermal imaging. Zeb had shot this guy, but if he had been detected earlier and if Broker had taken out the remaining ones, Zeb would have been fine.

Broker and Zeb had been very close, and Connor was amazed that he didn't show any trace of guilt or grief.

He had ventured this question to Bear and Chloe and then shut up, his ears flaming when they had turned cold empty eyes on him.

Broker had not let the Balthazars see Zeb's body – Clare had accompanied his body in an ambulance to the nearest hospital, where he was declared dead.

Broker had spent a lot of time with Rory in private, and Rory seemed to be the better for it. Connor and Lauren hadn't asked Rory what they talked about, respecting a newfound maturity in him.

Cassandra.

They had seen her just once since the rescue. Subsequently, lean, hard men had appeared, calm on the outside, with a don't-look-at-me-from-even-ten-feet-away attitude, cold-shouldering and ignoring everyone except those closest to Zeb. They had barred any access to her, taking her away from her apartment.

There had been a time or two when some of them had accosted Isakson, the FBI squaring off against some of the most dangerous men, but Broker and Clare had intervened and calmed the situation.

They had thought they had lost contact with Cassandra when the call came from her about the memorial service.

* * *

Connor stops his musings as he drives onto Park Avenue, heads toward the Church of St. Ignatius at 84th Street, and jams the brakes hard when he sees the crowd outside the church. A lot of those same hard men, but also many others, some old, a few teenagers, a few Asians and Hispanics.

'Have we come to the right place?' Lauren murmurs and then spots Broker, who is indicating some parking spaces far ahead.

As they walk back to the church, they're joined by Mark and Anne. Anne's eyes are red rimmed, and the usual spark in her is missing.

Taking in the crowd, she says, 'I didn't realize he knew so many people and had so many friends.'

'A lot of them must be his military buddies. The rest, probably their family and friends,' Mark and Connor reply simultaneously and then grin.

Anne holds Rory's hand. 'Are you okay, champ?'

He just nods, his gaze on Broker.

Broker greets them at the entrance and directs them inside. 'Cass is over there, waiting for you.' In reply to Lauren's unasked question, he adds, 'She's fine. She's a tough one.

'More important, how are you and champ here?'

Lauren smiles briefly. 'It all feels like a distant, horrible dream.'

Broker nods. 'Yes, and if you're feeling that, then you'll be fine. Just think of it as something unreal. And as for Rory, he'll be fine, too.'

They go inside the church, which is packed, a lot of ebb and flow around Cassandra, who's standing next to Clare and a couple of those hard impassive guys.

Connor feels awkward as they approach Cassandra and senses similar emotions in his entourage. It's the first time they've met socially since the rescue.

Rory rushes up to her and hugs her for all he's worth, breaking the awkwardness.

'This wasn't my idea.' Cassandra indicates the filled church once she, Lauren and Anne have shed a few tears. 'Broker insisted, and there were several others who came to me and said they would go ahead with this, with or without my permission.'

'This is Roger and Bwana. They were with us during our Catskills trip,' she continues, introducing two men standing next to her, one African-American, and the other, a relaxed Texan.

They both nod to Connor and his party.

'And this is Andrews. He was Zeb's handler at the agency.' She points to another, whose immaculate appearance doesn't mask hollow eyes and cheeks.

'Who are all these people?' Mark asks. 'I thought Zeb was a loner.'

'He was. Many of these people are those he helped, or families of those he helped over the years.'

'Over there' – she points to a teenage girl accompanied by her father – 'Dad owns a chain of retail stores in the Midwest. Daughter went to Mexico for a holiday and got kidnapped, with the kidnappers demanding a ransom. Zeb rescued her. There are many such people here. Zeb didn't know it, but all of them kept in touch with me.'

Cassandra smiles sadly and then chuckles at Mark's stunned expression. 'You really thought there would be about ten people or so here at the most, didn't you?'

'We all thought that,' Connor says before wandering away to have a look around and meet some of the people.

What feels like hours later, he turns to the lectern at the front as a hush falls across the hall.

Broker steps up, looks around, and chuckles. 'I think Zeb would be amused to know that so many had gathered in his memory. I'm sure he never thought he was that important. He would also shrug and think it was all just a waste of time. Thankfully we are all not Zeb.'

The room chuckles with him.

'But because we are all not Zeb, it's all the more important to pause from life and remember that there are these unusual people who impact our lives and change us. Today is not about mourning and not about Zeb alone. I am sure there are many more people like him that you might know. Today is about celebrating such people.'

He pauses and waits.

Silence greets him.

'You bastards, that was the cue for you to shout my name.'

Laughter fills the hall.

'Some of you will know this next speaker, though I'm not sure why,' Broker says, stepping aside.

A tall black man, distinguished looking with silver hair, fills the hall with his presence as a frisson of excitement ripples through the crowd.

Matthew Ferrer is widely regarded as the best Hollywood actor of his generation, with a worldwide following that even the Pope would envy.

'A few years back when I had won the Academy Award for *Forgotten*, I started receiving weird death threats, and my studio and my agent suggested that I seek personal protection. It did not sit well with me. Here I was, on top of the world, recognized all over the world, women chased me' – he paused – 'men, too.'

A ripple of laughter, the crowd hanging on every word.

'And suddenly, there were these crazies who seemed to be intent on doing me harm. Nevertheless, I took the advice of my agent and spoke to a few people; those few people gave me some names. I also spoke to the LAPD. The LAPD and quite a few of the others I spoke to kept mentioning one name, Major Zebadiah Carter. They also said he was not easy to get to and not very friendly.

'That suited me, that last bit. I had enough hangers-on in my life without a bodyguard looking at me with doe eyes. My agent called him; no response. I got the LAPD to call him; no response. I called him and left a message for him.

'He never returned my call, but one night after shooting on location in New York, he was sitting in my hotel room waiting for me, late at night. Boy, did that freak me out – this guy sitting Zen-like in my hotel room all dark, just looking at me, not uttering a single fucking word.

'"I want to hire you," I told him. "Everyone I have spoken to tells me you are the best personal protection guy out there."

'He just sat there looking at me. I'm sure you all know the Zeb look.'

A loud shout of assent in the hall.

Matthew takes a sip of water.

'I got him to talk somehow, or rather, he got me to talk and laid down the rules for working with him. Yes, me, Hollywood superstar, toeing his line. It was galling, I tell you, but my agent said I had no choice. Not if I was going to take those threats seriously.

'Zeb was my personal protector for three years, travelled with me all over the world, and saved me from a katana-wielding stalker in Tokyo, who just pounced on us when I was having dinner with my cast. That was some weird shit. Here we were having dinner in Tokyo's finest, the restaurant empty save for the cast, and then this guy bursts in through the door, yelling and shouting, waving a giant sword, nearly taking the director's head off. The guy jumped on my table, and then Zeb showed up, there was a blur, and next thing I know, the guy was hog-tied and Zeb was calmly sampling my dinner.'

His voice chokes.

'That was Zeb. He could slow time down. He taught me not to take myself seriously. That the world would not be permanently misshapen just because I was no longer in it.

'I have dined with presidents, met the Pope, romanced the most beautiful women in the world, but I have, I had, only one brother. Major Zebadiah Carter.'

A pin-drop silence and then a roar of applause washes over all of them. Connor notices that there is hardly a dry eye in the room, including his.

Much later, when they have sampled the hors d'oeuvres and Rory has spent time with Broker, Roger and Bwana, they make their way toward Cassandra, who is holding court in front of a long table.

The table has his ribbons and medals laid out: Purple Hearts, a Silver Star, a Medal of Honor – the stories behind the medals; a silver tankard, which Broker tells him is the Wimbledon Cup for long-range rifle shooting; and various commendations and certificates. At the other end of the table are a few photographs, Anne and Lauren gravitating toward them.

Mark, Connor and Rory look over the awards, reading the stories behind them, and move slowly to the photographs. He notices a curious stillness in the women, breaks off from the medals, and joins them.

There aren't many photographs. Just a few faded ones of Zeb when he was serving, a couple of them in either Afghanistan or Iraq or some dusty, sun-bathed land.

What has captured the women is a photograph in the center.

A clean-shaven, dark-haired handsome man, smiling, holds

a beautiful woman in his arms, both of them clasping a young boy – one of those pictures that arrests anyone by its vitality and grace.

Cassandra, her voice sounding far away, explains, 'He didn't tell anyone. Even here, less than a handful know – Broker, Bear, Chloe, one or two others, but no one else. He and his family were captured by terrorists when he was between assignments. His wife and son were tortured and killed in front of him. He couldn't do anything to help them.'

Chapter 20

He places the walnut stock of the M40 against his cheek, feels its familiarity settle in his hands, and sights down the rifle. The closed window of the apartment in a towering block opposite the street jumps out at him through his Leupold scope.

Broker and he have come to Rio hunting for Quink Jones, the last of the Rogue Six. He hasn't been that easy to locate.

* * *

Broker was able to trace him fleeing to Europe when Zeb took down Mendes, first touchdown at Amsterdam and then in Zurich, and after that the trail went cold. He had cajoled his databases, hacked into the most secure NSA systems, Interpol, everything that he could hack into, and still no sign of Jones. It was clear that Jones had realized the Rogue Six had a short shelf life and had decided to put some distance between Holt and himself.

However, no one could disappear like that, and his vanishing act gnawed away at Broker. Over a drink with Roger and Bwana, Bwana had joked, 'It's as if the critter has a new life,' and Broker had stared at him.

'Of course, that's it. The one thing Switzerland has, other than banks, is cosmetic surgeons. Jones has a new face and new identity.'

After that it wasn't that difficult for Broker.

Cosmetic surgeons in Switzerland who provided this service to terrorists, dictators, and assassins were not exactly thick on the ground. Armed with a reference from Clare, who was more than happy to make the hunt an agency one, the three of them had visited six clinics in Switzerland and at the last one had picked up the trail again.

Jones, with a new face and identity, had been renting an apartment in Copacabana, on Rua Paula Freitas, in a high-rise, the last few months. He had been leading a paranoid's life, seldom venturing from his apartment, and when he did, he moved erratically, seemingly without any plan – deliberately.

Broker and Bwana had spent a couple of weeks surveilling him and had then rented the apartment in the opposite high-rise, a little higher than Jones's but having a great view of his window.

The long gun was the easiest to get.

Broker's contacts in Rio had delivered an M40, with a

sleek, warm walnut finish that felt as if it belonged in Bwana's hands. A few days shooting and zeroing and they were good to go.

* * *

He has one shot at Jones, a window of opportunity of a minute at the most, when the target wakes up in the morning, pulls wide the curtains of his glass window overlooking the street twenty floors below, and spends exactly fifty seconds surveying the street.

This is the one thing he does regularly as clockwork every day in the otherwise unpredictable life he leads.

That window of opportunity is enough.

Bwana has taken more difficult shots than this, in more hostile environments than Rio de Janeiro. There was the one in Iraq where he had to take out a Taliban insurgent and had less than thirty seconds when the insurgent rolled down the window of his car to get some fresh air.

Zeb had been with him in Iraq.

The rifle is mounted on a tripod on a flatbed, well inside the apartment so that the muzzle flash will be undetectable from the outside or opposite.

He stops his mind from wandering, the clock running down in his head. He breathes deeply, slowing down his pulse, slows down his breathing, and makes life fade.

At exactly ten to eight in the morning, the curtains opposite and below are pulled open, and Jones's skinny frame fills the window and his scope.

Bwana waits two seconds to reconfirm the identity, and on the third second he sends the 7.62X51mm NATO round on its mission and sees Jones's head taken apart a couple of seconds later. As the body staggers back, he sends another two rounds through the center mass just to be sure.

He disassembles the rifle swiftly, yet unhurriedly, places it in a custom-made guitar case, wipes out all traces of his existence in the empty apartment, locks it behind him, and takes the elevator down.

At street level, he becomes one with the early morning rush, many heading to the beach, even at this hour.

Broker is smoking a cheroot, watching Brazilian ass go by, smartly dressed as usual, leaning against an anonymous saloon, when Bwana walks up to him.

'Grade A,' he says, waving the cheroot, and Bwana knows

he isn't referring to the cheroot.

Bwana grins, nods at Broker's unasked question, stows the guitar case away in the trunk, and they set off.

Broker takes a long detour that takes them to the seediest parts of the city, their destination being an illegal steel mill that reduces the rifle to scrap metal and the guitar case to ash.

It is evening by the time they reach GIG airport, return their car, and complete the formalities.

Broker looks a long time at Bwana, an oasis of stillness surrounding them amidst the hustle of the airport, knowing they will meet again, their paths will cross, and hugs him long.

Bwana, ex-Special Forces, brother in arms to Major Zebadiah Carter, Roger, Bear, Chloe, and Broker, walks away to Departures.

Bwana Kayembe, a warrior born in Luvungi.

* * *

Check out *The Reluctant Warrior*, Book Two in the Warriors series

www.amazon.com/dp/B00NJVZ9I0
www.amazon.co.uk/dp/B00NJVZ9I0

'*I just want people to read it and enjoy it as much as I have.*'
Arthur Livingstone, Amazon review.

'*Anyone who likes books by Baldacci or Child will find themselves enthralled.*'
Kathi D, Amazon review.

'*I dare you to try and put it down once you start it.*'
Monty, Amazon review.

'*Another great read from Ty Patterson, another Lee Child in the making?*'
David Hay, Amazon review

'*Patterson delivers stories and people I can relate to more than most writers in the genre.*'
Amazon review

'*Loved it – can't wait for next installment.*'
Tanya Schipelbaum, Amazon review

Bonus Chapter from *The Reluctant Warrior*

The boy woke up as soon as he heard his father stirring and peered out from under the edge of his blanket.

He saw his dad do his usual routine of looking across the small bedroom, from his bed tothe children's beds to see if they were awake, and then stepping cautiously to the window overlooking the street and scanning it.

His dad had been doing this for the last few months, and one day he'd asked his father what he was looking for. He had been brushed off.

They had moved to Brownsville not long ago, just over a year back.

For him life had been long periods of moving about, followed by short periods of stay and calm, and so far Brownsville had been one of those short periods of calm.

He looked across at his sister sprawled across the edge of her tiny bed, legs twitching spasmodically in response to some dream in her six-year-old mind. He wondered if she enjoyed moving so much; maybe for her it was normal, since she hadn't experienced anything else.

His eyes went back to his father still standing at the window – just on the inside, shielded from the outside – and wondered what he was thinking about.

He gave up after some time, sleep dragging him to oblivion.

* * *

Shattner knew his son was awake and watching from the changed timbre of his breathing, and knew his son was used to watching him at the window.

The apartment was just a single-bedroom apartment in Brownsville – a neighborhood well known for its crime in New York. This window was the only window that afforded him a view of the street below, and he could not avoid his son watching him.

Shattner stood in the shadows and watched life in the street pass. It had become second nature for him for as long as he remembered, to look out for anything out of the ordinary on the street before he stepped out. Nothing struck him, and he headed towards the door of the apartment. His son would wake up, make breakfast for his sister and himself, get both of them ready for school, and then the two of them would walk a couple of blocks to school.

After school, his son would collect his sister and do the routine in reverse.

By the time Shattner returned from work, his son and daughter would have finished their dinner and be ready for bed. Routine for many years.

His son, a mature adult in an eight-year-old body, had never experienced boyhood, had never enjoyed all the small things that childhood was about. For the briefest moment, the darkness of despair flooded his mind before he ruthlessly shunted it aside.

Later, when he was dressed and ready, Shattner stepped out of the apartment block, his eyes scanning casually as he walked several street blocks to the car-repair shop he worked in, on Blake Avenue.

He could have taken a bus to the garage, but he preferred the walk, even if it was a long one, since it gave him the freedom to observe anyone taking any interest in him.

His supervisor allocated him work as soon as he walked in – a Cherokee with a broken suspension, and that took up most of his day.

On returning home, he picked up the tail.

A short stocky man was trailing him from a distance. He was good, but Shattner at one time had done this for a living and sensed the tail immediately.

He sat down on a bench near Stone Avenue Library, bought some nuts, and ate them leisurely, taking the time to subtly observe the reaction of the tail and also to think the situation through.

The tail hung well back, and Shattner decided to do nothing about him. Those who employed the tail already knew where he was living and everything else about him. If he took on the tail, it would only tip them off that he knew.

He carried on home, stopping on the way to buy groceries. When he entered the apartment complex, he stood back in the shadows and saw the tail window-shop.

His apartment was on the third floor on Blake Avenue, in an apartment complex that housed many like him for who hope and a future was alien.

He could hear the excitement in Lisa's voice as she talked with her brother, the voices audible through the thin door of the apartment. He stepped in silently, and the world fell away as he saw his son and daughter doing their schoolwork on the table in the cramped living room.

'Daddy,' Lisa squealed as she rushed across the room and jumped into his arms.

'Shawn helped me with schoolwork.' Her voice came out muffled as she buried her face in his shoulder.

'Had dinner, princess?' He looked over at Shawn questioningly.

Both nodded.

'How was school, princess?' he asked her as he went to their small bathroom to shower and change. Over the noise of the shower, he heard Lisa recite her day.

Mrs. Harwood had awarded her a gold star for art. Michele, her best friend, had spilt milk on her uniform during lunch hour. Paul, that boy that Lisa didn't like, had called her stuck-up – at which Lisa had reported him to Mrs. Harwood. Shattner allowed her voice to wash over him along with the water, draining away his day, leaving him refreshed.

Lisa was jumping on her bed when he came out of the bathroom and leaped in his arms when he finished tidying up. He spent a long hour playing with her and then prepared her for bed.

She squealed in delight as he hoisted her on his shoulders and carried her to her side of the room and commenced reading her favorite bedtime story. She fell asleep during the second chapter, and silence fell over the apartment.

Shawn had gone to bed during the storytelling, had listened for some time before he, too, drifted off to sleep. Shattner sat with Lisa a long time, his mind emptied, before he roused himself and went to the kitchen to put together his dinner.

The way their routine worked, Shattner stocked up on all groceries and essentials during the weekend, and Shawn and Lisa fended for themselves during the week. The Office of Children and Family Services would not be happy if they knew.

'Dad?'

Shattner turned from the refrigerator to see Shawn tousled with sleep. 'Can't sleep?'

Shawn shook his head. 'Dad, will we ever have a normal life?'

Shattner heard the refrigerator door shut behind him, the soft thud drowned by the beating of his heart as he felt his son's eyes on him. A couple of long strides and he was crouching in front of Shawn.

'Two to three months at the most, baby. And then we'll be living like any other normal family. We'll celebrate birthdays, go on holidays, and have loads of friends...trust me, baby. Okay?'

Shawn nodded, his eyes dark, the faintest sheen of tears in them.

Shattner pulled him close and crushed him in a hug. It would not make up for giving his children a life on the run for eight years, but he didn't have anything else to give his son.

He carried his son to bed and sat beside him till his breathing slowed to a deep sleep. He checked his mobile, his only communication point, and saw a text message.

It was the one he was dreading.

'Tomorrow.'

No pleasantries of any kind. Short, terse, like the sender.

He thought he knew what the summons was about. He went to his gun cabinet – a grand description for a wooden drawer high up in the closet in the bedroom – and removed his Glock 30 and cleaning materials, and carried them to the drawing room.

He stripped the gun, wiped the parts clean, and then started a more thorough job of lubricating them. The smell of gun oil filled the room. A comforting smell, bringing back good memories. He assembled the gun, loaded its magazine, and chambered a round.

He didn't think he would need the gun the next day, but it never hurt to be prepared.

* * *

Author's Message

Thank you for taking time to read The Warrior. If you enjoyed it, please consider telling your friends and posting a short review. Word of mouth is an author's best friend and much appreciated.

You can find the reviews page by following the links on my author's page: *www.TyPatterson.com*

Sign up to Ty Patterson's mailing list and get the Kindle version of *The Warrior* free. If you tick the Launch Team check box, you will receive beta-read copies of all my new releases in advance, free.